KT-196-021

C155370324

It was no good fighting it.

What he hadn't offered in words she could see from the spark, feel from his increased respiratory rate. She was still thinking like a goddamned nurse. How long had it been?

Too long.

She'd managed to keep that bridge between her and intimacy for so long, fortified by Nonna's rules and ugly experience.

But what he was offering her—what she *thought* he was offering her—hot and quick—would take her off that bridge with a wide leap.

She'd spent ten years clinging on by her fingertips, frightened of what might happen. Of how much she'd have to give and lose all over again. But this was different. *He* was different. Max wasn't asking for anything but a good time—he wasn't the type to make promises or offer her any more. She'd been warned about that already. Which was fine with her.

So either she could go back to people she didn't know, in her cold, unfamiliar house, and spend the night alone with her memories—as she'd done for a decade—or she could take him up on his offer. One night of heat and fun and danger.

She could scramble back onto that bridge tomorrow.

The mojitos made her bolder. Instead of pushing away from him, as she knew she should, she held on to his arm and looked straight into his eyes. Made sure he got the message. What she wanted. Where they were headed.

Never had she felt so brazen, so alive.

Dear Reader

There are two reasons I particularly enjoyed writing this book. Firstly, I had the opportunity to work with good friend and wonderful writer Sue MacKay on the over-arching theme linking the two stories in *The Infamous Maitland Brothers* duet. With suggestions from our editors and lots of brainstorming we took a germ of an idea about feuding twin brothers and developed two intensely emotional stories.

The second reason I enjoyed writing this linked story is because it is set in a busy hospital, which is a new departure for me. The hospital is a fictional one, based in the centre of Auckland—New Zealand's largest city. Writing about twin brother doctors who are equally successful and important members of this hospital community was fun and challenging. Mitchell and Max have reputations as heartbreakers and neither of them is looking for commitment.

Transplant surgeon Max has had enough of people walking out of his life, so is reluctant to lose his heart to new nurse in town, Gabby. After a difficult past Gabby has moved to Auckland to reinvent herself, but she is not prepared for a life that involves falling in love… These two are so perfect for each other, but neither wants to admit it, so of course I had lots of fun helping them along a little!

I hope you enjoy Max and Gabby's story.

Warm regards

Louisa x

Book 1 in **The Infamous Maitland Brothers** duet
THE GIFT OF A CHILD by Sue MacKay
is also available this month

The Infamous Maitland Brothers is also available
in eBook format from www.millsandboon.co.uk

HOW TO RESIST
A HEARTBREAKER

BY
LOUISA GEORGE

All rights reserved including the right of reproduction in whole or in part in any form. This edition is published by arrangement with Harlequin Books S.A.

This is a work of fiction. Names, characters, places and incidents are either the product of the author's imagination or are used fictitiously and any resemblance to actual persons, living or dead, business establishments, events or locales is entirely coincidental.

This book is sold subject to the condition that it shall not, by way of trade or otherwise, be lent, resold, hired out or otherwise circulated without the prior consent of the publisher in any form of binding or cover other than that in which it is published and without a similar condition including this condition being imposed on the subsequent purchaser.

® and TM are trademarks owned and used by the trademark owner and/or its licensee. Trademarks marked with ® are registered with the United Kingdom Patent Office and/or the Office for Harmonisation in the Internal Market and in other countries.

Published in Great Britain 2013
by Mills & Boon, an imprint of Harlequin (UK) Limited.
Large Print edition 2014
Harlequin (UK) Limited, Eton House,
18-24 Paradise Road, Richmond, Surrey, TW9 1SR

© 2013 Louisa George

ISBN: 978 0 263 23851 8

KEN
ARTS & LIBRARIES

Harlequin (UK) Limited's policy is to use papers that are natural, renewable and recyclable products and made from wood grown in sustainable forests. The logging and manufacturing processes conform to the legal environmental regulations of the country of origin.

Printed and bound in Great Britain
by CPI Antony Rowe, Chippenham, Wiltshire

A lifelong reader of most genres, **Louisa George** discovered romance novels later than most, but immediately fell in love with the intensity of emotion, the high drama and the family focus of Mills & Boon® Medical Romance™.

With a Bachelors Degree in Communication and a nursing qualification under her belt, writing medical romance seemed a natural progression, and the perfect combination of her two interests. And making things up is a great way to spend the day!

An English ex-pat, Louisa now lives north of Auckland, New Zealand, with her husband, two teenage sons and two male cats. Writing romance is her opportunity to covertly inject a hefty dose of pink into her heavily testosterone-dominated household. When she's not writing or researching Louisa loves to spend time with her family and friends, enjoys travelling, and adores great food. She's also hopelessly addicted to Zumba®.

Recent titles by Louisa George:

THE LAST DOCTOR SHE SHOULD
  EVER DATE
THE WAR HERO'S LOCKED-AWAY HEART
WAKING UP WITH HIS RUNAWAY BRIDE
ONE MONTH TO BECOME A MUM

**Also available in eBook format
from www.millsandboon.co.uk**

**Praise for
Louisa George:**

'Author Louisa George fulfilled
the promise she made with her
emotionally satisfying debut offering,
ONE MONTH TO BECOME A MUM,
and took us to unexpected depths of
human relationship with
WAKING UP WITH HIS RUNAWAY BRIDE.
This story is a captivating blend of drama,
passion, emotional tension and romance.'
—*Contemporary Romance Reviews*

'A most excellent debut from Louisa George.'
—www.GoodReads.com on
ONE MONTH TO BECOME A MUM

PROLOGUE

'WE HAVE A DONOR.' Max Maitland put his hand on his brother's shoulder. A first step to making things right between them all. God knew, they needed it. That, plus a hefty dose of courage and his surgical skills.

Little Jamie's life depended on this being a success. Failure wasn't an option. Not now. Not when so much was at stake.

'Yes, we do have a donor.' Mitchell's eyes lit up with hope as they walked towards the nurses' station. 'Me.'

'What? No. There was an accident—the kidney's being flown in. We have to run some tests, but first thoughts are that everything's compatible.' Max couldn't risk his brother on the operating table too. 'I'll be the principal transplant surgeon, obviously. We're just waiting for the rest of the team.'

'No. I want to do this. I want to donate my kidney to my son. I have to do this, goddamit.'

Mitch's Adam's apple bobbed up and down as he swallowed. He gripped the edge of the desk, knuckles blanching.

Max knew how hard coming to terms with being a father had been for his brother. Harder still to learn the child he'd only just met would die without urgent help.

Dragging him away from the screaming telephones, the bleeping monitor and babies' wails, Max looked Mitch squarely in the eye. The steel gaze he knew was mirrored in his own eyes bored into him. Eyes so eerily identical to his. Maitland eyes. The same ones Jamie had. His nephew. *His brother's son.*

Max's chest tightened. How long had he wished for this kind of connection with his own flesh and blood? How many nights had passed in a fit of fantasy—about a family with people who cared, who believed in him?

Now Max could do something to make a difference, bridge that gap between himself and his estranged twin—make a real family. 'Are you sure? You know the risks? It's major surgery.'

'I know that I'm a positive match. I know that adult-to-child transplants work best. That living donors work better. I know I'd do anything. Any-thing. For my child.'

Max nodded. In the Maitland gene pool deter-mination beat anything else hands down. Stub-bornness came a close second, which meant he hadn't a hope of changing his brother's mind. But he had to try. 'Let's see what the tests show on this donor kidney. Then we'll take it from there.'

'No. Give it to someone else.'

'This is a good chance for Jamie. Donors are few and far between. At least wait and see…'

Mitch shook his head, sucked in air. 'Would you do that for your child? Would you wait to see if things panned out okay? To see if the higher chances of tissue rejection from an unrelated donor made him sick again? Watch him suffer when you could easily make things better for him? Or would you give him the best chance? Would you do it?' *For your nephew? For me?*

Mitch didn't have to say the words. Years of frustration and jealousy, anger and grief hovered round them tainted with the thick disinfectant smell that coated everything in the hospital ward. *Would you put yourself on the line for your fam-*

ily? Even if that family was something you hadn't spent a whole lot of time with.

Without hesitation Max answered. 'Of course I would. I'll make it work.'

CHAPTER ONE

THE SHED PUMPED with the throb of techno beat. A deep bass rhythm resonated off Max's ribcage, as if the music came from within him. Hard. Loud. Raw. Through a glass door leading out back he saw silhouetted people dancing, arms punching the air, the way he wanted to right now. The way he felt whenever surgery had been a success. But today—hell, nothing came close to that kind of buzz.

Mission accomplished.

Bill, the barman, nodded towards the bottles in the fridge. 'Hey, Max. Usual?'

'Sure. Line them up.'

'Celebrating?'

'I think so.' It paid to be cautious. The first twenty-four hours were often the decider, although with transplants the decider could be years down the track. He'd laid it all out to Mitch and Jodi, plain and simple; Jamie's operation had resulted in a functioning kidney, but a lot could still go wrong. Too much.

He didn't want to go there. Emotions had no place in a surgeon's work and in his career he'd always managed that—but saving his nephew's life? That was all kinds of different.

Bill slid the beer bottle across the bar, his eyebrows raised in understanding. The great boutique beer, plus the fact the staff never asked questions or gave advice, was the reason The Shed was Max's home away from home. After a heavy day of intense surgery he relished the chance to de-stress the best way he could in familiar surroundings, followed by some kind of hot physical workout—a bed was optional.

Here in the public bar there was no one save a couple from the phlebotomy unit and a single woman a few seats down with her back to him. A mass of thick dark curls covered her shoulders.

His gaze drifted down her straight back, stopping short at the taut line of the black long-sleeved blouse stretched across her spine. Her dress was more funereal than fun, so much so he wondered why she'd be in party central. Most girls here showed far more skin. Intrigued, his gaze travelled over the narrow dip of her waist. The flair of her skirt over a decent amount of hip. The right amount.

He imagined running his palm over those curves.

Running a cool hand over the back of his neck instead, he eased the tension in his shoulders. Man. After eight hours of surgery his hyped muscles needed a release. And he knew the perfect way.

A quick drink first. Then hit the back bar. Then…maybe…who knew? The night was still young.

'Barman? Excuse me? Hey.' The curls shivered as the woman raised her hand. 'Excuse me. Another mojito, please.'

Bill's pupils widened as he leaned across the bar to Max, his voice low. 'Been here an hour. Had three already.'

Following Bill's line of vision, Max caught a view of her face. In an urgent and acute response something twisted in his gut, tightened with an awareness that was full and powerful. Hell. It had been a long time since he'd had that kind of immediate reaction to a woman.

Her hair framed a soft face, kissable lips with a smattering of red lipstick. Almost perfect features—cute nose, a dusting of freckles. She was the kind of woman any man would give a second glance to. And most would chance a third. But the clip in her voice screamed that she was a woman not to be messed with.

So of course his interest ratcheted up the scale. Fiery women always presented a challenge. And, boy, did Max love a challenge. He hadn't become Auckland's most successful transplant surgeon without pushing a few boundaries.

Okay—a lot of boundaries.

She caught him looking at her but he refused to look away.

Her eyes. Wow. Large, dark, almond-shaped, glittering with something. Hurt? Anger?

Which in itself was a warning sign. But, hell, a conversation didn't mean a whole lot of anything. And if it went further—he'd lay out his intentions from the get-go. Starting with nothing deep and meaningful. Ending with don't ask for forever.

Max leaned across the bar to Bill. 'Is she waiting for someone? Been stood up?'

The barman shook his head. 'Nah. Don't think so. She hasn't checked her phone or looked at her watch.'

Good. Not stepping on anyone's toes. He didn't

break that brotherhood code as easily as others. As easily as Mitchell had. Max raised his beer to her. 'Tough day?'

'And getting tougher by the minute.' She took her refreshed drink and turned her back to him.

'Okay, I get it. You don't want to talk, right?'

Swivelling round, she gave him a full-tilt death stare. Definitely anger in her eyes. Hurt was a distant cousin. 'Gee, whatever gave you that idea? Very sorry, but my back's not feeling very chatty tonight.' She turned away again, but not quite as far as she'd gone before.

'Watch you don't get whiplash with all the swivelling around.' He caught her profile. The uplift of her chin. Tight lips.

And very possibly the hint of smile.

He'd been on the verge of leaving, but the fading smile reeled him in.

Never one to admit defeat, he slid into the seat next to her, determined to make that smile last a little longer. 'It's okay. We don't have to talk.'

'Get out of here. Really?' Her ribcage rose and fell quickly as she turned to face him, slim fingers running a diamond locket along a thin silver chain at her throat.

Her dark gaze slid from his face down his body

and back again. 'People actually say that? Is it from *Cheesy Pick-ups for Dummies*?' She held up her hand. 'Wait. No. It's a phone app, right? *Lame Lines for Getting Laid.*'

'Ouch. Cruel. I'm mortally wounded.' He touched his heart for effect. 'Actually, it's from *Just trying to be friendly dot com*. But forget it. I'll leave you in peace.'

She blinked. 'No. I'm sorry. Come on, hit me with another line.'

'That was my best shot. I'm all out.' He winked, took his phone out and whispered, 'Quick. Help me out here. What was that app called again?'

'Yeah, right. Like you'd need it.' She laughed. The glitter in her eyes turned to one of humour. Her mouth kicked up at the corners—she was fighting it, but he'd made her laugh. And that gave him a sharp punch of pride to his gut. She clearly got a kick out of the sparring and, hell, judging by the effect of that smile on his libido, so did he.

Her eyebrows lifted. 'You must have some more lines? Surely? Tell you what—you try them on me and I'll rate them out of ten. Then no other poor unsuspecting woman has to put up with the bad ones.'

'Okay.' He took a slug of beer and rose to the

bait. If it meant a few more minutes laughing with her, then game on. Then he'd go out back. 'My friend's all-time favourite was "Hey, darling, do your legs hurt from running through my dreams all night?"'

'No. No. No. Stop. Running away from a nightmare, more like.' She grimaced and put her fingers in her ears. 'That's terrible. A very poor three. Please don't tell me people actually use that?' Her head tipped back a little as she laughed.

He was mesmerised by the delicate curve of her throat. Imagined placing a kiss in the dip lined with the silver chain. When she leaned forward again he got a delicate scent of flowers. Made him want to inhale way more deeply than he should.

Boy, he definitely needed to get out more.

She shook her head. 'Was that your best shot? You are so bad at this.'

'Thank God, I've never needed them. Obviously.'

'The worst one I ever heard was "Is your dad a baker? Because you've got a nice set of buns."' She snorted into her drink, then pointed to her face. 'Hey. Eyes up here.'

'Clearly he was a good judge of…character.' Max reluctantly dragged his gaze from the swell of her blouse-covered breasts back to her smiling mouth. Whatever shadows had been haunting her when he'd arrived had gone. Her eyes shone clear and bright. Job done. 'Seriously, you just looked like you could do with cheering up.'

'And you voted yourself cheerleader? How sweet.' Her eyes narrowed and she pointed at him. 'But I was managing just fine without the benefit of your help. Now you should go. Thank you.'

Huh? This was new. He hadn't been knocked back for a very long time.

Adrenalin pumped round his veins. Instinct told him they could have fun together—and his instinct was rarely wrong. That and the fact he always liked to win meant he'd have to up his game. The chase usually lasted all of two seconds once they knew who he was, what he did. 'And yet here you are, *smiling*…er?' He held out his hand. 'I'm Max.'

'Max…' She paused, clicked her fingers together. 'Max…Max Maitland. You're that guy. Thought I'd seen you before.'

'Seen me where?' Because he sure as hell hadn't seen her. He'd have remembered.

'I had my first-day orientation on the paediatric high dependency unit today. While you were doing your rounds I looked after little Jamie for a few hours. He's gorgeous.'

'Yes. Yes, he is.' A weird tightness squeezed his chest. He breathed it out, chalked it up to the long day. He'd just left Jamie sleeping soundly in his mother's arms, tubes and drains permitting. He'd looked so small, still a baby really. Renal failure sucked at any age—but at three? The world wasn't fair. He quickly checked his phone. No messages. No news was good news. 'He's my nephew.'

'I get that. Same name. Same eyes. Cute kid. That must have been hard, watching your nephew fighting for his life then having to operate on him. Takes guts.'

The guardedness she'd had in her eyes relaxed a little as she watched him. She held his gaze as if weighing him up—no, more, as if she could see right through to his core. A hazy connection snapped between them—he sensed she under- stood some of what he'd been through.

Weird. The women he usually met only wanted a good time, a turn on his boat, expensive din- ners, the high life of a successful surgeon. None of them ever saw past the label and the cash. Cer- tainly none of them had X-rayed his soul before.

Her lips formed a small pout. 'You did good today. Very good.'

He leaned in. 'That's because I am good.'

'Now, that's better. Rising up the scale, Mr Maitland—maybe an eight.' Raw need flared behind her gaze. Her lips parted a little as she ran the tip of her tongue along her bottom lip.

This was dodgy territory.

Mixing business with pleasure was a definite no. Too much gossip, too much to live up to. Hell, he'd had enough of that.

And yet…there was something simmering between them. A tension building, an awareness they both acknowledged, if not with words then with those fleeting looks. Like a gathering storm, intense, alive with static.

Then the connection fractured as she frowned. 'But I know all about men like you. Big-shot surgeon. Work too hard. No time for friends or relationships.' She glanced at his hand. 'No wedding band. No one to go home to—or you'd be there already. You just want something quick and hot and uncomplicated.'

And now she was stamping on a raw nerve. No woman had ever challenged him so blatantly.

Pure lust fired inside him. He whispered in her ear. 'You reckon you fit the picture?'

'Not today. So if you don't mind, I need a little privacy.' She held her glass out to Bill. 'Another one, please.'

Max didn't want to ask why she was so intent on getting tanked. The woman was free to do what she liked. She certainly looked as if she could handle herself. In truth, the less he knew about her the better—that way things could stay strictly professional.

But his interest was way off the scale.

He wrapped his hand over her wrist, gently pulling the glass onto the bar. His fingers were drawn to her hand. He turned it over and rubbed her palm with his thumb. Checked for wedding rings. None. Good. The static jumped and buzzed around them at his touch. 'Don't you think you should be slowing down?' And why did he care?

Her fingers shook free and the frown deepened. 'Seriously? I've had four drinks. I can still walk, talk and count. No big deal. Don't bust a gut over me. This is a once-a-year indulgence I allow my-self. I'm having a ball, so don't go spoiling my party.'

He wanted to ask why. Why once a year—

what had happened? Why here? Why the hell had things aligned for him to bump into her today, when he needed something, as she'd so rightly said, hot and quick. With her it felt complicated already, not least because they were going to be colleagues. And there was that thing…that invisible tug between them. 'Hey, I'm a transplant surgeon. Livers fail. I worry.'

'Oh, sweetie. Don't.' Her mouth twitched. 'Once a year. The rest of the time I'm a saint.'

'Well, lucky I found you tonight, then. Your liver will be eternally grateful.'

'Sure it will. But my brain will never forgive you.' Gabby shook her head. The man was beyond irritating. Okay, she conceded, and not a little gorgeous with his dark messy hair, tight black jeans and startling blue eyes that drew her gaze every time she looked in his direction. They were a deep-set, mesmerising, intense blue framed by eyelashes bordering on illegally long.

Not to mention the way his white shirt clung to thick biceps and broad shoulders dragging her eyes to his body.

She tried to ignore the fire smouldering in her belly as he touched her hand.

But really? The man was rude and way too self-assured. Six feet plus of trouble.

His reputation went before him—first time she'd had an orientation that had come with a health warning—Max Maitland, legendary surgeon, serial heartbreaker.

If she hadn't seen the softening in him at the mention of Jamie she'd have believed the hype—chalked him up as a self-centred charmer.

She had to admire him, though. He could spar as well as she could. But his ego was spilling out of that crisp cotton shirt. From previous ugly experience she'd erased over-confident and über-charming from the list of qualities she liked in a man. Nonna had been right about one thing, men just couldn't be trusted.

She rolled her eyes. 'Next time I need some advice from the fun police I'll know who to call.'

'And I'll make sure I'm right there in my superhero outfit.'

'I so did not need an image of you with your undies over your trousers.' She shrugged, stifling a laugh, trying hard not to look at the way those jeans hugged his long legs. His perfect backside. Fascinating.

'It's the twenty-first century. We don't do out-

fits like that anymore. I'll let you into a secret…'
He finished his beer. 'We *transform*.'

She mustered indifference, holding her laugh
back. 'I'm only interested if you transform me
another mojito.'

'A virgin mojito for sure.' He motioned to Bill
to bring an alcohol-free drink despite her protests.
'Er… I still don't know your name.'

'You are very annoying.' And damned gorgeous,
and way off-limits. And all the things she'd been
warned about. And funny and sexy, too, and there
was that strange pull to him that she was trying
to ignore. But they were going to be working together so he'd find out her name soon enough.
'Charge Nurse Radley. Gabby, to my friends.'

'Well, Gabby, pleased to meet you.' He stuck
out a hand. 'Do you have any interesting secrets
you'd like to share?'

Not even if hell froze over. She'd moved to
Auckland to restart her life, not relive it. Free-
dom. At last. Space of her own. No one to tell her
what to do.

She regarded his hand with as much disdain as
she could muster. God, she'd met her match here.
Most men had run a mile by now.

In another life this could be fun. He could be fun.

Dodging his question, she bristled. 'Like I said, you don't get to call me Gabby. I'm Charge Nurse Radley.'

'*Gabby*. So that is Gabrielle? Gabriell*a*?' His grin widened as she stuck her tongue out. It was as if he knew exactly which buttons to press, and definitely how to tease. 'Ah, Gabriella, your eyes give so much away. Nice name, and I'll stick with Gabby, thanks.'

'Are you this forward with everyone or is it just me?'

'Considering it's your first day in a new job, I'd have thought you'd want to make a good impression.' He laughed, his chin jutting up. 'Here's a hint—you could make it easier for people to get to know you.'

'I do, usually. Just not people like you.' And not today, when she just wanted to be left alone. 'Don't worry, I can do professional and competent. Tomorrow.'

'I can't wait. Any more frostiness and we'll need to increase the central heating. I'll make sure I pack a scarf.' He checked her half-empty glass and then his watch. His smile turned from friendly to insanely wicked. '*Gabby*, you've got the wrong impression of me. Or you're delusional.

Or drunk. Whichever, clearly you're a danger to yourself. So, if you're done, I'm taking you home.'

'Whoa, buster. You are not.' She'd had enough of people telling her what to do. 'I'm not ready to go home…' She paused.

Home? Where the heck was that? Certainly not the new shared flat she'd dumped all her boxes into yesterday.

Or Wellington, with its bittersweet memories and dark, dark corners.

But she'd determined not to think about any of that. Apart from tonight. The whole day had been exhausting—a new job, new people. A sweet baby fighting for his life. Piling a tumult of more emotions to the anniversary she kept, like a vigil, every year.

And now Mr I'm-sexy-and-I-know-it was piggy-backing on it. Adding a hint of danger to the heady cocktail of anger and hurt.

'Thank you, but I'm fine on my own.' She dragged on her jacket, lost her balance and slid off her chair, slamming into his hard wall of stom-ach. 'Oops.'

'Are you sure about that?' His voice sent a breeze against her neck followed by ripples of something hot pattering through her stomach. 'Because if there's anything I can help you with…'

Well, she had been sure. Sure she wasn't tipsy, sure she was going to walk away.

But now? Not so much. Maybe the mojitos had made her a bit woozy after all. She wasn't used to drinking, to meeting men in bars. To the dizzy lights of a strange new city, or the safe embrace of a man like Max Maitland.

Strong arms circled her waist as he hauled her upright and led her outside into the dark street. Heat fizzed through her body. His smell, woody and heady, washed over her. She put her hands out to his chest to create space, but something held her there—her body flat refused to move. A wave of awareness jolted through her.

As her gaze travelled up his chest, over his too-damned-sexy mouth and up to his bright blue eyes, she realised it was no good fighting it. What he hadn't offered in words she could see from the spark, feel from his increased respiratory rate. God, she was still thinking like a god-damned nurse. How long had it been?

Too long.

She'd managed to keep that bridge between her

and intimacy for so long, fortified by Nonna's rules and ugly experience.

But what he was offering her? What she thought he was offering her, hot and quick, would take her off that bridge with a wide leap. She'd spent ten years clinging on by her fingertips, frightened of what might happen. Of how much she'd have to give and lose all over again.

But this was different. He was different. Max wasn't asking for anything but a good time—he wasn't the type to make promises or offer her any more. She'd been warned about that already. Which was fine with her.

So, she could go back to the people she didn't know in her cold unfamiliar house and spend the night alone with her memories. Like she'd done for a decade. Or she could take him up on his offer. One night of heat and fun and danger.

She could scramble back onto the bridge to-morrow.

The mojitos made her bolder. Instead of pushing away from him, as she knew she should, she held on to his arm and looked straight into his eyes. Made sure he got the message. What she wanted. Where they were headed.

Never had she felt so brazen, so alive. 'Actually, I can think of a few things I need help with.'

'Then I'm your guy.' For a second he seemed to still, confused no doubt by her see-sawing signals. Then heat ignited in his pupils. He tipped his head, his mouth a fraction away from hers.

An ache spread from her abdomen to her groin, rushing through her blood to every nerve ending. When his hands reached for her waist and pulled her closer she stepped into his arms, pushing away any negative thoughts.

When his thumb rubbed against her hip bone her heart rate spiked. Then his mouth was covering hers with a force she'd never experienced before.

She wrapped her arms around his neck, deepened the kiss, opening her mouth to his tongue. His hardness pressed between them and she rocked against it. The desire he'd unleashed in her only seemed to grow more intense as she curled into his heat.

She didn't know where this temptress act was coming from. Something about Max Maitland made her feel so sexy—and knowing it was for one night only, she played along. God, if her nonna could see her... No. *No. No.* She hauled

Max closer and lost herself in his heat, erased any thoughts of home from her brain.

Shivers tingled down her spine as he cupped her face and crushed his mouth to hers.

Eventually he pulled away, his breathing ragged. 'Okay, *Gabby*.' Still keen to play games with her. Good. She wanted to play. 'You want to rate me now?'

She pretended to think for a moment, pressed her lips together—relishing the unfamiliar stinging sensation from his kiss. 'Nine.'

'Nine?'

She bit her bottom lip and leaned closer to his ear. Breathed in the scent that had started to drive her wild. 'Okay, nine point five.'

'Really? And I lost half a point for what, exactly?'

'It didn't last anywhere near long enough.'

CHAPTER TWO

'I CAN REMEDY THAT.' Max's forehead rested against hers, his breathing finally steadying. He'd met his match here. Hallelujah. Things could get very interesting between now and tomorrow morning. 'I'm not back on duty for a few hours. You?'

Gabby frowned. 'Early shift. And as it's my first day in charge, I have to make an impression—so watch out, Mr Maitland. I can be ruthless.'

'Woo—scary nurse lady.' But, yes, they would be colleagues from tomorrow. Damn. This was getting too complicated. He hesitated, his judgement getting the better of him. And his conscience too.

He didn't know her—but what he'd seen so far was that no matter how much of a front she put up, she had shadows, and a past—or else why would she be in the pub on her own, hell-bent on getting wasted?

And he didn't want to veer into that kind of territory.

But she was intriguing. Strong and strident one minute, sexy siren the next, and all the time with an undercurrent of vulnerability that tugged at his protective instinct.

And right now he wanted to bury himself inside her. Not just anyone. Not someone. Her.

'Hey.' She kissed him on the cheek. 'Earth to Max.'

'You want to talk about why you were in the pub?'

'No. I don't want to talk at all. Don't ask me anything, and I won't ask you.' She placed her finger to his lips. 'You don't want more. And neither do I. So forget the sensitive-guy thing.'

'But…?'

'But nothing. Tonight we are…friends. Tomorrow we are co-workers. I can cope with that if you can. Seriously. Cross my heart.'

Her fingers tiptoed down his shirt buttons and she drew a cross over his heart. When she peered up at him through thick black eyelashes he caught the flash of desire in her eyes. 'Now you are severely dropping in my ratings. If you want to get back up to at least a seven, you've got a bit of work to do.'

'Seven? How did that happen?'

She wiggled her hips against his thigh. 'You, Mr Maitland, are all talk and no action.'

'You want action? Right.' Max walked her across the deserted street and into his apartment block. Crazy stuff. He never offered his place. One of his rules, and he had a few—no staying the night. No promises of anything. Anything. No sharing his private cave. That was way too personal—and he didn't do intimacy on any level, not if he could help it. But his apartment was close by. And what they needed right now was hot and quick. He punched 'P' and the lift jolted.

'You live in the penthouse? Wow.'

'Sure. You have a problem with heights?'

He couldn't resist the smile. It had taken a lot of damned hard work to earn enough to get this place—but it had been worth every hour and every cent just to see the look on his uncle's face. 'We could go back to the ground floor. I own an apartment there too—but it's rented out at the moment—could be a bit crowded.'

'Now you're just showing off.'

'Oh, believe me, I haven't even started.' He nibbled her ear and watched her squirm with delight further into his arms. Her scent coated everything—her hair, her skin—his skin. And it fired a zillion nerve endings in his groin.

He swiped his card and opened the apartment door, activating the lights.

He couldn't help the smile when Gabby gasped. Whether it was at the one-eighty-degree view of Auckland's glittering night skyline or his kisses on the back of her neck he didn't know. Either way, with her sharp intake of breath he was all turned on as hell. He took her hand and led her into his space.

'Wow! Look! The lights. You didn't even touch a switch.'

He laughed. 'There was me thinking my kisses made you gasp.'

'You really do have a high opinion of yourself, don't you?' But she traced a finger down his cheek and over his lips. 'Do it again.'

He waved a hand and the room plunged into darkness again. 'Like that?'

'Oh, yes.' Palms worked their way down to his chest.

Then the lights came on again.

Then off.

Then on.

She grinned as he caught her, her arm in mid-air. 'Oops. In the real world we have flicky switch things. This is so cool.'

As the room plunged into darkness again he found her mouth, the pressure of her fingers on his back stoking the fire in his belly. He guided her to the couch, raking his hands through those thick curls he'd been aching to touch all evening.

With every stroke of his tongue she moaned with pleasure, sending him dangerously closer to the edge. He undid the buttons on her blouse, slid his hand under her bra, felt the delicious contraction of her nipples against his palm.

He struggled with an intense need to take her. Here. Now. But he sensed he needed to take it more slowly with her. *Wanted* to take it more slowly. They only had a few hours before morning and he felt as if time was running out. If he hurried, the magic would be lost too soon.

When he pulled away slightly he watched her face transform from beguiling to bewitched as she gazed across the room to the city view.

'This place is freakin' huge! Incredible! Look at all those lights, the harbour. I can see a cruise ship down there in dock. It's magical.' Then she glanced around the moonlit room, her delight evident, like a kid in a sweet shop. 'The glass... so much glass...must cost a fortune in window cleaning.' She laughed, ran her hand along the top of the couch. 'And all these white fixtures, the blonde wood...but no knick-knacks? Pictures? Photos?'

'No.' He wouldn't explain.

'What about Jamie? Your family? You must have photos of them.'

'I don't like clutter.' He'd managed to live like that for a long time. No mess—physical or emotional. 'I keep things simple.'

'I see. Noted.' She paused and seemed to take that in. Then she nodded, understanding his hint not to probe further. 'It's stark, but breathtaking. I've never seen such a space. It's like something out of a magazine.'

'*Metro House Monthly*—February edition.' At her frown he explained. 'The interior designer was pretty happy with it so she booked an editorial. There's a spa, too, out there in the garden.'

'You have a spa and a garden all the way up here? Oh. My. God.' She ran to the Ranchslider doors but he flicked the remote and they opened before she got there.

'Oh.' Disappointment laced her voice as she stepped out. 'That's not a garden, it's a desert. There's nothing here.'

'I don't have time to look after plants. I hardly have time to sleep these days.' He tutted, took her hand and walked her across the empty decking space towards the spa.

Looking at it all through her eyes, yes, it was kind of sparse. Just how he'd planned it. Uncomplicated, stress-free.

Just like Gabby seemed to be. Instead of all the pretence that he usually went through with women—the faux affection, the predictable seduction, the craning of their necks to see the colour of his credit card before they said yes—Gabby seemed undeniably, ruthlessly real.

Her bright-eyed reaction to his apartment was genuine, not greedy. She'd been honest about her expectations. And flirty and unexpectedly fun.

A pinky-orange glow shimmered across the balcony, illuminating the red and gold highlights in her hair, her dewy skin, warm eyes. She fitted perfectly into his arms, soft curves filled with promises.

No, it wasn't his flat that was breathtaking—

Gabby was. How amazing to make love with her out here in the moonlight…in the spa.

Anywhere.

She leaned back against the railings, her forehead crinkled with frown lines. For a moment he felt like he'd disappointed her, but then she smiled. 'If I lived here I'd have an oasis—somewhere I could come sit and read, relax. A sky garden with lots of plants. A home isn't a home without flowers and plants.'

Where's home? The question almost tripped off his tongue, but he remembered their agreement— no questions. His hands ran over her shoulders, down her triceps, and he realised she was shivering in the early-winter breeze. He locked her into his arms. 'I'm not into flowers and plants. That's girl stuff.'

'No. Real men get their hands dirty.' Taking his hand in hers, she examined it. 'You've got surgeon's hands. Wow. Just think of all the lives these hands have saved.' She pressed her lips into his palm, kept her eyes locked with his, then slowly placed his hand over her breast. Went up on tiptoe and filled his mouth with her tongue.

Maybe this was a dream. A post-surgery dead-on-his-feet hallucination. A beautiful woman. A still night. Promises... Anytime soon and his cell-phone was bound to go off. He was going to wake up.

On paper she was his perfect woman: she didn't want a relationship, didn't want more than one night. Was happy to forget it all tomorrow. Just like him. Sure, on paper she was perfect, but there must be a catch. There was always a catch. 'Are you for real?'

'No, I'm a figment of your imagination. Open your eyes and I'll disappear in a puff of smoke... gone...' she whispered, and giggled.

'Then I'll keep them shut. I don't want you disappearing on me. Not just yet.' He kissed her again hard and fast, cupping her breast. Her excited moans of pleasure spurred him on. Just the simple act of kissing her was a sensual feast that he didn't want to end. Her hips ground against his and suddenly a fire blazed in his groin, hot and hard. Tearing at her straps, he removed her top, lifted her bra and took one nipple into his mouth.

Watching the reaction on her face—concentrated joy—spurred him to give the other nipple the same treatment.

She clutched at his hair. 'Oh, God, this is so good. I don't suppose this place has a bedroom?'

'I have three.'

'Goody. Which one do we start in?'

Her skin against his mouth fired spasms of need through him. He dragged his lips from her shoulder. 'Master. Now.'

'Don't stop, though. Don't stop.' Ignoring her groans of protest, he took her hand and led her into his bedroom. 'Wow. Just when I thought things couldn't get any more impressive.'

As she pointed to his bed he was hit with a surge of pride. Okay, so it was a handcrafted masterpiece, imported mahogany, Egyptian cotton. Yeah, it was impressive.

But when she said, 'It looks so perfect I daren't mess it up,' he swooped her into his arms and lifted her onto his bed—her dark hair instantly flaming against the white linens. Her skirt ruched up to her hips, revealing long shapely legs.

Palming her thigh, he joined her on the bed. She edged closer, fitted into his space. Kissed him again, soft and sweet. Then in an electric moment the tension ratcheted, the kissing became more frenetic, the need more explicit.

He slipped her skirt off, kissing across her bellybutton down to the edge of her panties. 'How am I doing on the rating front?'

'Oh…nearing eight…' she breathed out on a sigh.

'Only an eight? I show you this…I do this…and this…' He moved back up to her neck, nibbled her ear, slicked a slow trail from her lobe. Tweaked her nipple again with his hot mouth. 'And I only get an eight?'

'Hey, a guy's always got room for improvement.'

'We'll see about that.' Grabbing his condoms from the bedside-table drawer, he paused and looked at her. Realised he didn't want hot and quick. Wanted long and slow. And maybe again tomorrow.

He shook those kinds of thoughts from his head—useless and pointless. People walked through his life, no one ever stayed for long. That was how it worked for him. And for Gabby, too, it seemed. 'Are you sure?'

Placing her hands on his chest, she frowned. 'I want you to know this is not something I've done in a very long time. I don't usually…you know… do this… I am on the Pill but, yes, definitely use a condom.'

She seemed hesitant. Maybe the alcohol was wearing off. Good call—he wanted her head to be in full working order if they were going to do this. No regrets for either of them. He brought her fingertips to his mouth. 'It's okay, you know. I could take you home. We don't have to do this.'

'Oh, yes, we do. You promised me hot and quick.' Gabby's courage had begun to waver, but her need to have him hadn't diminished. No, siree.

Running her hands over his back towards his waist, she pulled him to her and crushed her lips against his. A surge of heat spiralled through her from the small of her back to the top of her head. Mr I'm Sexy was so different from any other man she'd kissed. Not that there'd been many—she'd made sure of that.

Dumb, really, that on today of all days she was doing this. When she should be staying away from any kind of risk. But the headier the risk, the more her body wanted to take it. Take him. Now. And nothing was going to stop her finally taking something for herself.

Because, for the first time in forever, she felt absolutely, totally free.

Scragging his shirt over his head, she slicked kisses down his hard chest, over a smattering of hair, across hard muscle. He pressed against her as he shucked off his jeans. His hands grasped her hips, slipping off her pants, fingers reaching her inner thigh.

For a moment she stiffened, worried about what could happen. If she even knew what to do now. If she would be enough for him. What would happen afterwards. Tried to put out of her mind what had happened last time she'd done this.

But unlike last time she wasn't an innocent grasping at a fairytale, looking for an escape and dreaming about happy ever after—this time she knew exactly where she was headed. Sex. Need. No promises. No illusions. She was a woman, powerful and in control.

His hands stroked her skin and it felt as if he was stroking her insides too. And she wanted more. His kisses heated her. Banished the cold she'd felt for so long. Stoked the fire that raged from her belly to her breasts and that didn't stop…couldn't stop…wouldn't stop until he was inside her.

Then there he was, edging into her, telling her to relax, calling her beautiful over and over. Until she truly believed she could be. His breathing quickened and his words stopped, and all she could hear was their sighs and the thud of her heart and the blood pounding round her veins.

Until he took her over the edge, and all sounds splintered into one explosion of shuddering joy.

A perfect ten.

A harsh, tinny tune jolted Max awake. His first instinctive reaction was to feel across the duvet for the uncompromising Gabby.

His second was to reach for his phone.

God, he was doomed.

And she was gone. He'd opened his eyes and she'd disappeared, just like she'd promised. Which irritated him more than it should have. Most women wanted him to stay, had always been put out when he'd made up his excuses and left.

He'd never had the time or the inclination to invest in anything longer than a fling. And he'd certainly never given any woman time to do the walking—he'd had enough of people he loved disappearing from his life already.

But the room still smelt of her scent. The sheets did. And so did he.

His phone blared again.

Focusing on the lurid green message, his heart began to race. Jamie.

A rising temperature less than twenty-four hours post-op. Dipped urine output. Distressed kid.

Within minutes he was on the HDU, trying to keep his voice in check so as not to spook Jamie's mum, Jodi. He scratched his head as he approached the bed, still unused to her being round again after so long.

It was weird enough when Mitch had dated Max's ex. But even more awkward to have her back in his life, at his work after so long. Not that anything lingered between them anymore, except his wish they could all move on. But Jodi's hurt was still there, along with his brother's betrayal. Unmentioned. Unresolved. Like everything with Mitch.

His attempts not to growl at the surgical on-call house officer disappeared along with any trace of post-damned-fine-sex good humour.

'I need full blood and urine screens, swab drain and catheter sites, keep an eye on central venous pressure and his blood pressure. How long has his temp been this high?'

'An hour, maybe two.'

'And you waited to tell me. Why? I said I was to be contacted immediately if there was a change in his condition.'

'I thought we could control it. I was hoping the paracetamol would hold it in check.'

'Since when does paracetamol hold an infection in check? You wanted to mask the symptoms and not investigate them. Pretend he hasn't got a problem, right? Great.' God, he was surrounded by...

He took a breath. It was the middle of the night. They were tired. He was tired. And poor Jamie. Thick, dark shadows edged the little boy's eyes as he stared up at them.

Max's heart squeezed. He never allowed himself to feel anything but professional concern for his patients. But Jamie? Jamie was special. He was the sticking plaster they needed to stick them all back together. They hadn't come this far for the kid to get sick again. Not on his watch, anyway.

He should never have left them this evening. Even though he'd been exhausted by the surgeries and countless demands on his time.

He shouldn't have gone to the bar. Even though he'd left clear and strict instructions with his staff.

He shouldn't have taken Gabby to his apartment. Just in case something like this happened.

So that was a mistake he wasn't going to repeat. He didn't need a hefty dose of guilt to add to his conscience.

Although Jodi was a doctor, he tried to explain the turn of events in everyday language. Knowing that in the middle of a long night, with spiralling concern, technical terms wouldn't be much use.

'Jamie's got a spiking temperature. Which could mean one of a few things. Pneumonia, urine infection or just something sticky at the drain sites.'

'Or it could be rejection, right?' Her palm covered her mouth as she held in the tears Max knew she wanted to shed.

Accelerated acute rejection—death of the kidney soon after operation. He didn't want to imagine it.

He put a reassuring hand on her shoulder as he would with any other patient's relative, but did she think that was strange coming from him? So far he'd played out the ex card pretty well, but everything normally clear-cut had become muddied. He focused instead on upholding his professional manner. Hiding behind that was preferable to dealing with emotions.

'It's a very real possibility, but he has a reasonable urine output. We're doing a blood scan and antibody check. Honestly, it could be anything. It's quite common to have some sort of low-grade infection post-op. So we'll increase the antibiotics and titrate his fluid input. That should keep him comfortable.'

'Okay.' Jodi's lip wobbled as she looked equally uncomfortable. 'Er…thanks. For everything.'

'Hey, it's my pleasure. Anytime.' Although heading up the team operating on his twin brother and his nephew in a double-whammy of transplant surgeries was a one-off he hoped never to repeat.

As he injected more antibiotics into Jamie's Luer, Max dredged up a smile for Jodi. 'How's Mitch doing?'

'He's fine. He was wheeled in for a few minutes to say good-night to Jamie, but he was wiped out after his operation so he went to sleep. He says to say thanks, mate.'

Mate? Since when was he his brother's mate? Maybe they were finally getting somewhere. Such a shame it had taken something so drastic to get them talking again. Max huffed out a breath.

Jodi managed a tired smile in return and he felt a strange pang of regret. Not of losing her—because she had been so wrong for him and so right for Mitch—but because he'd never seen anyone have that love-filled, misty-eyed look over him.

Must be getting soft.

'You look bushed. Why don't you have a lie-down?' He dragged over a foldaway bed, grabbed some pillows and covers, and made her sit down. 'Get some sleep. I'll stay right here with him.'

'But what about his temperature? Or if he cries?' She was terrified and exhausted and what she needed was a rest, away from the eternal twilight of the hospital ward. A foldaway bed was the closest he could come to providing that.

Not for the first time he wished he could do something, anything, to prevent his estranged family from suffering through this.

'Then I'll wake you up. Trust me. We'll be fine.' Resisting an urge to drop a kiss on his cute cheek, he scruffed the boy's hair instead. Keeping a lid on his emotions at work was his mojo—and he intended to keep it that way.

The boy murmured a little but finally went back to sleep, leaving Max in the cold silence with too many thoughts.

Too many worries about the fate of this little chap.

Too many guilty stabs about where he'd been and what he'd been doing instead of keeping watch over his family.

Too many memories of a pool of thick black curls, a sarcastic mouth.

And a very sexy smile.

CHAPTER THREE

'HE'S HAD A LONG and difficult few hours, so don't wake him.' The night charge nurse finished her handover by parading the whole of the day staff in front of cubicle four.

Gabby's chest did a funny little hitch at the sight of a sleeping Max. Slumped half on a chair and half on Jamie's bed, he was completely and utterly comatose. And with stubble on his proud jaw he was completely and devastatingly gorgeous.

God. She glanced round at the rest of the crew. Could they all tell? Did she have 'Guilty' written all over her face? Did her smile scream *I've just had fabulous sex with Mr I'm Sexy here*?

She tried to make the smile more interested in the handover than the subject, as the unfamiliar ache of bedtime gymnastics thrummed through her body.

Bad, bad girl. Maybe her nonna had been right all along. She waited for the thunderbolt her grandmother had promised. The dark satanic music as she was dragged away to the bowels of hell.

Nothing happened. Gee—what a surprise.

If sex was so bad, why had it felt so good?

Her palm found its way to her throat. She tugged on the necklace she refused to take off. She knew exactly why.

Concentrate.

How would she ever concentrate with Max there?

'Where's Jamie's mum?' she whispered to the night nurse, dragging her eyes away from Max. God, he'd been amazing. She'd been amazing— and that threw her even more. She didn't know she could be like that.

'Mr Maitland sent Jodi home at five-thirty, once he'd got Jamie's fever under control. Said she needed a good rest and a hot shower. He's been here ever since. Wouldn't leave him. Wouldn't even let go of his hand.'

Gabby's heart constricted as she noticed the tiny hand wrapped in Max's fist. No. *Harden up, Gabby.* Don't get involved. Don't let a little boy tug at your heart. Or a grown man snag a piece of it.

Hurriedly closing the curtain and shushing the

staff away, she took a moment to compose herself. Tried to think through the thud of her alcohol-induced headache and the wave of lust fizzing all the way down to her knees. She'd allocate Jamie to someone else. That way she wouldn't have to spend any more time with Max or his family. No looking into too-blue eyes that made her feel weak. Then she'd avoid him, for the rest of her life.

The sluice was looking pretty attractive right now. The treatment room. Cleaner's cupboard. Africa…

Coward.

Sure, sleeping with him had been epic. Fan-bloody-tastic. The best and most wild thing she'd done in a decade. Liberating. Affirming. Crazy. But now?

Not so much.

She didn't regret it, though. It had been one amazing night that she'd always treasure. But focusing on him took her brain power away from the things that mattered—her new job, her future. Putting the cloistered past behind her. And that included Max and his far-side-of-minimal apartment. She refused to let everything go to hell again because of a man. Especially a man like Max Maitland.

She found one of the house officers loitering too near the biscuit tin at the nurses' station. 'Hey! Hands out. Are they clean?'

The HO snatched his hand away from the chocolate digestives and looked down at his fingers. 'Er...yes.'

'Makes a nice change.' She refused to smile. She would start as she meant to go on. Her reputation as efficient and no-nonsense had preceded her. Give them a smile and before she knew it there'd be chaos...and no biscuits left. Every hospital ward was the same—the doctors always devoured the biscuits. 'And you're waiting here for...?'

'Mr Maitland's ward round. It started five minutes ago but he's not arrived. That's not like him. Should I call him?'

Cripes, and it was her job to accompany the ward round too.

So much for her well-constructed avoidance plan. 'I'm sure he's very busy and has just been held up. He'll be along in a few minutes. Why don't you chase up those blood results for Peter Brooks in the meantime?'

It was no sin to fall asleep when off duty but no

doctor would want to be found sleeping on duty, even if he'd been up most of the night.

Scanning round for someone to go wake him up, she saw a very organised ward—her new staff all working under her strict instructions, getting patients up and washed, doing pre-op checks, dressing changes, no idle chit-chat. A hive of activity that left no one, *no one* else she could ask to stop their work and go and wake Mr Maitland.

That was the first time her efficiency had been back to bite her in the backside.

One steaming mug of coffee and a round of toast and jam later she dragged open the cubicle curtain. 'Max? Mr Maitland?'

Placing the tray on the over-bed table, she bent to his ear. Resolutely did not breathe in that delicious smell that had driven her wild and that she'd been reluctant to shower off only hours ago.

Did not look at the stubbled cheek she'd dropped a kiss on as she'd left.

Did not allow herself any spare emotions other than that she was very busy and he was taking up her time. 'Oi! Maitland, wake the hell up.'

'Lovely to see you again, too.' He lifted his head from the sheets, creases streaking down his cheek. The sweet curl of his lips made her heart hiccup in a peculiarly uncomfortable way. She'd kissed that mouth. It had roamed over her body into places no one else's mouth had ever been. That mouth had given her so much pleasure she felt the heat seep into her cheeks at the memory.

But there was a line between kissing and fun and a bit of *harmless* sex, and the cold harsh reality of relationships. Harmless sex? Boy, she'd been dreaming that day ten years ago. And after her heart had been shattered into too many pieces she'd made sure she kept on the right side of that line.

Even though last night she'd tested it, seen how much the line could bend, nothing Mr I'm Sexy could do would drag her to the dark side.

He sat up and stretched, glanced over at Jamie—satisfied himself with his observation—and then turned back to her. 'So you didn't disappear into thin air after all, Gabby. Here you are. Lovely... and fresh...and...so loud?'

'Busy ward, Mr Maitland. Busy day.'

'After what you did to me last night you can definitely call me Max.' His smile morphed into that wicked look he'd had in the bar. 'How's the head? How are you?'

She so did not want to have this conversation.

'Fine. Now eat this. Quickly. Your ward round was due to start fifteen minutes ago. We need to get a wriggle on.'

And they'd done a lot of that last night, too. Her cheeks blazed.

His mouth twitched. He rested his chin on his hand and held her gaze, his eyes misty with sleep. His hair was dishevelled and annoyingly perfectly ruffled. Sex hair.

It would be so easy to just lean in and kiss him again. But she pushed the plate towards him instead. 'Hurry up. I haven't got all day.'

His hand covered hers. 'Not before we clear the air.'

'Nothing to clear.' She twisted her hand out of his grip.

'You sure, Charge Nurse Radley? You were an animal. I particularly liked that thing you did with your finger—'

'Do not…' His proximity was jangling the one nerve she had left. First proper day in charge and she did not need this distraction.

She glanced over to make sure Jamie was still asleep. Peered out through the curtains to see if anyone could hear.

The patient in the next bed grinned at her and

waggled his finger. Gabby silently wished the poor sick teenager a swift dose of short-term memory loss and dodged back behind the curtain.

She jabbed her filed-to-a-sharp-point fingernail into Max's chest. 'Okay. You. Me. Sluice. Now.'

'But I've got a ward round.'

'Coward.'

'Never, ever challenge me like that. Because I have no fear, Gabby.' His words breathed down her neck as he followed her into the sluice and closed the door.

Trapped. In a small, hot room. Alone. No, not alone—with six feet three of glorious out-of-bounds hunk. 'You want to taunt me some more? Just to see?'

'I am a professional person trying hard to get a little respect around here. You do not talk to me like that when there are patients close by.'

'So I can talk like that now?'

'Absolutely not.' Her mouth tipped into a smile. She tried to stop it. Bit her lips together, tensed the muscles, but the smile kept coming. 'And I was not an animal.'

'I meant it in a good way. Uncaged, wild.'

He leaned against the steriliser, folded his arms, his legs crossed at the ankles. So relaxed that clearly the one-night thing was a common occurrence for him. She'd probably been just a notch in his magnificently handcrafted bed. She'd bet anything his heart didn't pound and skip and jitter like hers did.

His eyes pinpointed her, fixed her to the floor. He started to lift his shirt up, inching very slowly over that fine line of hair that pointed straight down towards his zipper. She swallowed through a dry mouth. Watched as centimetre by centimetre his abs then pecs were revealed.

His voice was hoarse and inviting. 'I'm sure I've got scratches on my back. You want to check?'

'No, I do not. Put yourself away.' *Before I jump your bones.* 'We're not going to talk about this again. Okay? That person you met last night? That's not me. That was a different Gabby.'

'Not the real you? You seemed very real. You felt very real… Oh. No…the animal thing…' He hit his head against the steriliser. 'Please, God, don't tell me I've woken up in some sort of paranormal universe? You're not going to go all weird or hairy and shapeshift on me?'

Laughter burst from her throat. 'No. I was just drunk, which is a rarity. Thank God.' She'd been bewitched by Max, or the mojitos. Either way, she wouldn't be giving a repeat performance. And she would never ever drink again. No matter how much she wanted to forget. She pointed to her scrubs. 'This is the real me. This is the only Gabby you're going to know. At work. Charge Nurse Radley.'

'Which is a damned shame all round.'

Yes, it was. 'And now we go out there and pretend we don't know each other at all. At least, not in the biblical sense.'

'Right.' His teasing grin told her he could pretend all she liked. But he knew her. *Knew* her.

'Right.'

'Excuse me…' The door swung open and Max Maitland walked through it. She did a double-take. Talk about a paranormal universe.

Max leaning against the steriliser, all cocksure and oversexed.

Max standing at the door in pyjamas, wheeling a drip that was attached to his arm, pale and tired-looking.

The in-patient one was minutely shorter, had longer hair and an air of worry around him. Unlike the doppelgänger in the corner. He was just downright smug. Or had been. His jaw tightened.

'Whoa.' She'd heard they were brothers, but no

one had mentioned identical twins. How could there be two such beautiful men in the world? It made her head spin.

And did Max Two have the same freckle just above his...? Could he make her gasp and moan?

Stop.

She banished such thoughts as she held up her palms. 'This is weird. Can—?'

Her Max was by Max Two's side in a second. *Her Max?* What the...?

His cocky demeanour evaporated into concern, his voice lowered. 'Are you okay? Who said you could leave your bed, Mitchell?'

'I did.' Max Two glowered.

'I was going to come and check on you. You should have waited until the ward round.'

'I was told you hadn't even started it. I came to see Jamie...' He gripped the drip pole as his jaw tightened to exactly the same tension as Max's. 'In case he needed anything.'

So alpha clearly ran in the family. She wanted to tell him that Max had spent a good part of the night looking after that scrap of life out there. And was running late because of it.

But she held her counsel. 'Would anyone like to introduce me?'

Max turned and smiled. 'Yes. Sorry. This is my brother, Mitchell. He was the transplant donor for Jamie. He's also consultant ED specialist here when he's not on the dark side. Mitch, this is the new paediatric HDU charge nurse, Gabby.'

'Gabby. Hello.' Mitch's eyebrows rose as he looked from Max to Gabby then back again.

There was a distinct edge between the brothers. So close in appearance, but a gulf stretched between them.

Oh, she knew enough about families that things didn't always run smoothly, that there were crises and ups and downs. Hell, she knew you could be angry and disappointed with someone for years and years, but you still had to treat them with respect.

Because they were family.

And family, she'd had drummed into her, was everything. Which was why things had turned out so perversely in the end. Why she wasn't going to have one of her own. Because now she'd wrested some control into her life, she'd never give it up.

But this Maitland thing seemed different. The brothers stood aloof, distant. There was a strange cold charge between them. And yet a child's life hung in the balance out there. More than anything that should count. Surely they should be united in that?

Mitch nodded towards her. 'I came to find out who's looking after Jamie today.'

'I allocated him to Rachel. She's very competent. Last thing I heard she was just about to give him his breakfast. Why don't you come and see him? He's probably ready for some daddy hugs. Then perhaps we could alert your nurses to your whereabouts.'

She ushered them out of her sluice room. As things had been progressing with Max in a way-too-dangerous direction, Gabby was thankful for the interruption. But perturbed by the existence of not one but two very distracting Maitlands.

Surely to God one was enough.

Six hours later Gabby finally found a moment to breathe. Slumping into the soggy orange sofa in the ward staff lunch-room, she broke out her sandwiches and yoghurt and started to eat.

Luckily the ward round had run smoothly. Jamie appeared to be making it through his first day post-op with just a niggling temperature. And there had been no major events.

Apart from her near heart attack every time

Max brushed past her on the drug round, at the nurses' station, along the corridor. Was it normal for a doctor to spend so much time on one ward?

Of course it was—he was dedicated, hard-working. And always, it seemed, there.

'Gabby? We meet again.'

There. See? Always there, his deep voice making her stomach do cartwheels. She swallowed her mouthful of tuna mayonnaise. 'I'm just leaving, actually.'

'No, you're not. Your feet are tucked up, your shoes discarded across the floor, you're only halfway through a magazine and if I know women well…' He let the *'and I do'* hang in the silence. Well, hell, he certainly knew how to please a woman, as she'd learnt last night. 'You won't go until you finish the article on best celebrity diets.'

He squished down onto the cushion next to her, mug in hand. The fabric of his scrubs stretched tautly against the muscle of his thigh. The thigh she'd caressed, gripped and, by all accounts, scratched. She dragged her gaze back to his mouth, his words. 'Which means, Gabriella, that we have time for a quick chat.'

'I don't think so.' She made a big deal of slipping her feet into her shoes, checking her watch, weighing up her options. Still ten minutes of her break left. She could leave now and attend to the piles of paperwork or she could last out her break. With him. In here.

She felt the heat in her cheeks and knew her stupid body was betraying her. What to do? 'I told you, Max. I'm not open to that.'

'To what?'

'More of last night. The whole sex thing…'

'Yes. No. Me too. Although…I could be persuaded. You have to admit it was good. We were good. Anytime you want a replay, I'm your man.' His eyes glinted and he appeared to be holding back a laugh.

Annoyingly, she liked it when he laughed. His whole body lit up and his attention focused totally on her. Made her feel he'd laughed just because of her. This was why she didn't date. Didn't want to get caught up in the lure and charm of someone like Max.

He leaned forward a little. 'Don't look so worried. I was only going to let you know I'm off to my outpatient clinic. Jamie's temp is still wobbly, so I'm going to arrange for some more scans to double-check everything. Should be later today.

In the meantime, if you need anything, call the house officer.'

'Oh. Okay. Of course, that's fine. And I'll personally check Jamie's obs.' She managed to bluff her way through her embarrassment.

Of course he'd put their night behind him. He was a player. And at work. She'd already given him the brush-off and he'd moved on. A guy like Max wouldn't ask twice. Didn't need to—there would be plenty of other offers. The gossip machine whirred with his and his brother's sexual exploits. 'How's Mitchell doing?'

His eyes darkened and his back stiffened at the mention of his brother. She got the impression that, like her, he didn't talk about personal stuff. Even if personal stuff included a patient and a member of hospital staff.

'Mitchell is fine.' He stood to leave, but paused. 'I think I might need to apologise for him.'

'For what?'

'Let's just say that tact isn't his forte.'

'Believe me, I don't think anything you Maitland brothers do could shock me. Your reputations go before you.'

Because once she'd discovered they were identical she'd made it her business to discover as much about them as possible. Didn't want to find herself propositioning the wrong brother!

She knew about Max's history as a heartbreaker, sure, and there were lots of women queuing up to try to cure him of that. What she hadn't expected to hear was that he and Mitchell had barely spoken a word to each other for the last few years they'd both been working at the hospital. That some kind of feud boiled between them, making communication on any scale largely impossible. That no one really knew why.

No matter—she didn't need to know much past who to call in an emergency. She tore off the top of her yoghurt and licked the lid.

Max grinned, reached across the back of the sofa and stuck a spoon into her yoghurt pot. Ignoring her whack on the back of his hand, he licked, eyebrows peaked. 'So I have a reputation?'

'Oh, yes. Big and bad.'

'Tough job, but someone had to do it.' He perched on the edge of the sofa arm and finished the rest of the yoghurt she held out to him.

'It depends if good-time guy and commitment-phobe float your boat.'

'What can I say? Having fun isn't a crime.'

'Not just you—your brother too.' She didn't

even try to lose the laugh. 'So who's the oldest? You or Mitchell?'

'Me. By twenty minutes.'

A blink of an eye really, and yet the responsibility clearly sat heavily on him. Operating on his younger brother's son must have played a part in the wisps of grey at his temples. Made him look sophisticated, self-assured. Belied the playful spirit she knew lurked underneath his professional mask.

'You must have had a lot of fun growing up with a twin. I always wanted a sister, someone to talk to. I've heard all sorts of stories about twins. Swapping clothes. Swapping girlfriends. Conning teachers. Secret languages...'

The grin slipped. 'We weren't close.'

'How so? That's unusual for twins. Were you always vying for position? Too much competition?'

'Geography.'

And with that he shook his head and left the room. It was as if a switch had been flicked. All his good humour and good manners had instantly evaporated, leaving her feeling uncomfortable and strangely bereft.

What did he mean? Geography? The academic subject? Or geography as in distance?

It didn't matter and it certainly wouldn't have any bearing on her professional relationship with him. And she really shouldn't care.

And if she did, it was only her innate reaction that a human being could look so hopelessly, horribly lost—if only for a second.

Before he'd managed to pull up the barriers again.

CHAPTER FOUR

So, HE'D SAID more than he should have. That was the trouble with sleep deprivation—it did funny things to a man's brain.

As did beautiful women. He usually handled it, no problem. But Max couldn't put a finger on what bothered him so much about Gabby Radley. Sure, she was distractingly beautiful. But he'd taken gorgeous women to bed before and had never sought them out the next day.

And she was funny. But he'd met plenty of amusing women.

It all came back to the way one look of hers could pierce his soul.

In the staff room she'd only been making polite conversation. She hadn't attached him to a lie detector and demanded answers. And yet for the first time ever he'd felt like talking about his past. About the way things had careered out of control, about everything he'd lost. And had never got back.

No matter. He'd survived so far—excelled, in fact. Spilling his guts to a woman wouldn't change a thing.

He exited the lift and huffed out a long breath. The day had melted into forty-eight hours of constant demands, an unexpected death, dealing with a grieving family. The gut-wrenching reminder that life was so fragile.

All he needed was a shower and bed. Where he could put everything out of his mind. Focus on rest and getting ready for more surgery tomorrow. Ensuring Jamie got better. Putting things back together with Mitch. Forgetting Gabriella.

Gee, there'd been a time when he'd had no one to think about but himself. *Be careful what you wish for.*

Turning the corner towards his apartment, a flash of colour grabbed his attention. Scarlet in the midst of the carefully designed neutral palette. A splash, vivid. Bright.

Weird. He got closer. A plant? A red plant. In a black ceramic pot.

Not a pretty plant either—this was gnarled wood, browny-green leaves, a bunch of itsy red petals. He picked it up and examined it. It had a strange smell.

Why the hell would anyone leave him a plant?

Shrugging, he let himself into his apartment where the fading remnants of Gabby's fragrance hit him square in the solar plexus. Between her and the plant they were going to fumigate him out of the penthouse.

He held his breath as he placed the plant on the kitchen bench. Stepped back. It didn't look right—too much red.

Moved it to the dining table. No.

The coffee table. No.

It was too eye-catchingly bright, a misfit, chaotic in the sea of…in Gabby's eyes, bland. God, now he was looking at everything from her perspective too. He really needed to stop that.

He didn't notice the note until he'd put the plant outside on the deck. Hoping for out of sight, out of mind.

Max,
I'd rate your so-called 'garden' a woeful one.
   And that's only because it's so cool to even have a garden at twenty thousand feet. Here's something to help it rise up the scale.
Charge Nurse Radley

He smirked and began jabbing numbers into his phone. Made a few calls. On the last one she picked up. 'Hello?'

'What the hell am I supposed to do with this... monstrosity?'

'Good evening to you too, Mr Maitland. It's a geranium. They're very popular in France. People put them in window boxes.'

He heard the laughter in her voice and immediately relaxed. 'If I did that and it fell off the railing, it'd kill someone. It's a long way down.' He peered down to the city street hundreds of feet below. 'Why are you giving me lethal weapons?'

'It's a flower, but you're a guy so everything has to be a weapon, right? It was more about encouraging you to take time out to smell the...er, geraniums. Besides, it's a sin to live anywhere where there aren't flowers.'

'Looks like I veered deep into the dark side, then. I'm good at that.'

'I know.' There was a catch at the back of her throat. Sounded a lot like the sighing noise she'd made the other night when he'd kissed her. Then her voice crackled back down the wire, softer now. 'Hey, I heard about your day.'

'Yeah? It happens sometimes. We lose the ones

we don't expect and sometimes the sickest ones pull through.' Exhaustion washed over him. It was never good to let his guard down, to share the toll a day like this took on him. Much easier to push it all deep inside into a hard, tight knot and hope it didn't get so big it strangled him.

All the time he'd been working on the kid he'd been silently thanking anyone who'd listen that it wasn't Jamie who was dying. What kind of a doctor did that make him?

Hell, it made him real. An uncle, with people to care about. But for the first time in decades he'd had a taste of what families must feel like, waiting, praying, hoping. So losing a child so soon after working on Jamie had hit him hard. 'I'm a last-resort surgeon. I get them when the only alternative is nothing at all.'

'I heard you wouldn't give up, though. I heard you did what you could and more.'

'Sometimes it just isn't enough.' But if he thought like that he'd never get up in the morning. Years of wishing he'd fought harder against his uncles and more for his brother had only given him a steely determination never to give up. And never to get close enough to anyone to care about losing them. Because, damn it, that hurt.

Her voice brightened a little. 'Okay, so here's the deal. Stick your nose close to the flower and take a big breath right now.'

'Why?'

'Do it.' Now she had that take-no-crap charge-nurse voice again. 'Now.'

'Okay. Okay.' He inhaled. Coughed. Stepped away from the plant. 'Ugh.'

'Now breathe out slowly. Geranium oil is supposed to help with stress and anxiety.'

'I'm tired, not stressed or anxious. At least I wasn't until I found a plant on my doorstep. I suppose you'll want me to look after it. Water it? It's like having another mouth to feed. Suddenly I'm responsible for another life. God, the pressure.'

That she'd even thought about the impact of today's loss struck a chord. Never mind that she'd left him a present. He heard her laughing, imagined the way her head tipped back, the light in her eyes. Remembered how she'd been out here, hot and hungry, on his balcony. How soft she'd been in his arms. How good a rerun would be. 'I do know a really great way to ease tension. Works every time.'

'Back to that again? No, Max. We agreed.'

'You agreed. So you get to have your wicked

way with me, and then…that's it? I'm dumped?' He laughed. He was never the dumpee. It didn't fit right and he didn't much like the prospect. In far too many ways. 'You're as bad as me.'

'We both took what we needed, no questions asked. So, yes, I'm the same as you, Max. If that's bad then so be it.'

'Hmm. I like bad. Bad is good. And if we're so similar you'll know exactly what I'm thinking. Right. Now.'

'No. Hush.' It was part warning, part dare.

'Yes, Gabby. I'm thinking about how good we were. How it's even better that neither of us wants anything more than sex.' At the word 'sex' he heard her swallow, her breathing becoming rapid and heavy. Imagining her reaction fired his testosterone surge into hyperdrive. 'How good it would feel to do it again. Now.'

'We can't. I—'

'Where are you?'

'At…home. In my room. Trying to unpack. Finally.'

'I can be there in ten minutes.' He couldn't have her here again. Bad enough he'd broken that rule already. Bad enough he'd have the damned plant around, invading his space. 'I'm very good at un-packing.'

He was?

'No! You can't come here. Just stop. Please, this is ridiculous.' This time panic coated her voice. She clearly didn't want him invading her space either.

Why not? Did she have the same personal code he did? Or was it something else?

And that was none of his business.

He heard a shrill landline phone ring in the background. Voices.

'Mum. No. Of course I'm not avoiding you. I've just been busy. Just wait…I'm on the other line. What? For goodness' sake, I told you I don't want to talk about that ever again. You promised me. No. No. *Wait*. Don't cry. Please. I'm sorry, I know. Yes. I'm sorry too.' Then Gabby came back to him. Harassed didn't describe it. 'Max, I have to go. It's my mum.'

'Call her back.'

'No.'

Hell, if he had a mother to talk to he'd put her way up the priority list, too. And if she was cry-ing he'd be there like a shot. 'Then call me back when you're done. Because I'm not done.'

'No.'

Then there was silence. Apart from the hazy noises of the city street. And nothing, but a bright flash of red in a pretty dull landscape.

And a whole lot of questions he wasn't allowed to ask.

The key to one-night stands was to walk away and not give a damn.

So Gabby had heard.

So she'd failed miserably from the start. Despite the bravado and the very frequent use of the word 'no', her body wanted to scream *yes, please* at every Max Maitland encounter. Which was becoming tiresome in the extreme.

Ten days later and she was bordering on lust exhaustion. But not for much longer.

'There we go, no more spaghetti to get tangled in. All ready for your transfer.' Gabby removed the last of Jamie's tubes and checked the dressing on his supra-pubic incision, just below his belly button. His little hands clutched his dad's and, as instructed, he hadn't moved. Hadn't whimpered or cried. Just stared up at her with wide, trusting eyes.

She allowed a ripple of tenderness to flutter

round her heart. Wondered how things might have been different…then locked that thought away. No point in dwelling on things past. She'd made her decision and lived with it knowing it had been the best thing she could do. No matter how much it hurt.

But it was always so good to help the littlies get better. Just so very hard to let them go. 'You're pretty much all fixed up, little man. Just wait for Mummy to come back and then we can all go over to the paediatric ward together.'

And that would mean no more Maitland eyes staring at her from every corner of the room. Not Jamie's, his dad's or his uncle's—all too blue, too bright and too alluring.

'Urine output still okay?' Having let go of his boy, Mitchell stood at the end of Jamie's bed, his eyes fixed on the four-hourly observation charts. Gabby took a chance to have a closer look at the twin brother that Max had no pictures of. That he refused to have a dialogue about.

They were breathtakingly similar. She couldn't imagine having someone else just like her in the world. It would be disconcerting. Could they read each other's thoughts?

Perhaps that's why they'd had such a rift.

She considered asking Mitchell about their history—but, heck, it was absolutely none of her business. She'd be mortified if anyone pried into her past. 'It's so great he's off the critical list now, and his urine is absolutely fine. Liquid gold.'

His eyebrows peaked. 'Never thought about it like that before. Pee has really just been pee until now. Having a kid is a real wake-up call.'

'I can imagine. But don't worry, everything's fine. Blood pressure's normal. Blood tests are within normal limits, that wobbly temp was just a blip. But they'll keep monitoring everything on the ward and slowly bring you all up to speed with the anti-rejection drugs, so you know what to do when you get home.' As she spoke she felt a blush start from her cheeks and spread. Fast. The guy was an ED specialist. He'd know the routine better than her. 'Oh. Gosh. I'm sorry. I'm just trying to… You're a doctor…'

'Hey, I'm a dad first. Which took a bit of getting used to.' He peered at her and chuckled. The first time she'd seen him smile since she'd started working there. Parental responsibility hung heavily on him.

Her heart ached to think how much that burden could be shared if he and Max were on better terms. 'You're looking much better, too. It'll be nice for you to get back to a normal family life at home. Try to keep him quiet for a while, though, he's still got a lot of healing to do.'

'Keep him quiet? Clearly you've never tried to parent a three-year-old.' Mitchell laughed, meaning well. But she felt her shoulders stiffen and the familiar emotions roll over her, slamming her heart against her ribcage.

Determined not to dwell on the past, she feigned busy-ness. After the last phone call with her mother she resolutely would not talk about it. Ever. Again. And that meant here. With her new friends. 'Well, if you don't mind, I'd better get on. There's always a pile of paperwork for transfers.'

'Hey, Charge Nurse Radley, all organised for going to the ward?'

She hadn't seen Max arrive but now he was there his voice soothed her nerves. Deeper and warmer than Mitchell's, it never failed to send shivers of something shooting through her. This time it was like balm to a burn.

She inhaled deeply and kept things professional. 'Sure. And now I have phone calls to make.' She gave them both a stern, matronly smile. Avoidance plan reactivated. The less time she spent with

Max the better. Maybe then she'd get over the lust exhaustion more quickly.

Max nodded towards his brother. 'Mitch. You look much better.'

'Thanks.' Mitchell opened his mouth to say more then closed it, obviously changing his mind.

Communication between the two of them was robotic, only saying what was absolutely necessary. Brothers didn't act like that. Strangers did. People who had nothing to say to each other. Surely, after a lifetime they could show a little more warmth? And yet she could see in their eyes that they were both aching to reach out.

Almost two weeks of caring for Jamie and she'd barely heard a word between them. Interfering wasn't her style, but they needed a damned push. 'You two are priceless, you know that?' She stared at them both in turn.

And kept the simmering desire for Max in check. Yes, she'd kissed that stroppy, grumpy mouth. Yes, okay, if called to account she'd admit she wanted to do it again. And again. Either that or slap it.

And she really should not be checking out his backside in those scrubs. So, yes, she was all kinds of confused.

But one thing was very clear: after all the reports of how Mitchell and Max had been before the transplant she would not have her ward turned into a Maitland battlefield. 'It's great that Jamie's fixed up and on the mend. But for his sake you two could try being a bit friendlier to each other, especially when you're in front of the little guy. What kind of message do you want him to grow up with?'

'Sure. Sorry.' Mitchell scowled, picked up his son and squeezed him close. 'Look. Here comes Mummy. Time to get going. Wave goodbye to Gabby.'

The kid waved his chubby hand and beamed. 'Bye, Gabby.'

'Okay, I'll catch you up once I've got the forms.' As always she held tears in check. Something about a cute toddler hit her full-on hard in the chest every time. They had that earthy, homey smell that drew her to sniff their heads. Huge eyes that showed every emotion. That little-man swagger—half baby, half toughy. All cute, and feisty, and enough to make her heart ache.

As she prepared to leave, her attention was briefly captured by Max's reactions to Jodi. He nodded towards her then turned away, unable, or unwilling, to hold her gaze. Gabby wondered whether it was her imagination or did he seem tense around his brother's girlfriend too?

Something was very wrong with this family set-up and gossip or no gossip she needed to find out what. If only to produce harmony in the hospital corridor.

'You be good now, Jamie. I'll be down to check on you very soon.' As Max pressed a knuckle to the boy's cheek, uncharacteristic tenderness flitted across his face. And swiftly on its heels came a blanket of indifference. Emotional shutdown.

She recognised it because she'd seen it in her mirrored reflection all too often.

Then he turned and walked back to the desk at the far end of the ward.

After she'd completed the transfer, Gabby offered Max a seat in her office and sat opposite him, keeping the large mahogany desk between them as a buffer. 'I know I'm way out of line here, but do you want to talk about what's going on with Mitchell?'

'What?' He shrugged.

'The monosyllabic communication. It's like working with automatons.'

'It's just brother stuff, you know how it is.'

'No, actually, I don't. I'm an only child.'

He laughed, pushing a hand through his hair, his mouth kicked up into a half-smile. 'Praise the Lord for that. I couldn't handle two of you.'

'Well, welcome to my world, Maitland One.' This was way off professional limits and she knew it. But she couldn't bear to see families fall apart. She'd been there. Was the poster child for how to stuff things up.

And ever since she'd hated seeing people tear each other apart when they should be loving, supporting, talking. Hell, it might be too late for her, but it didn't have to be that way for the Maitland men.

Infusing her voice with as much understanding as she could, she leaned across the desk. 'You want to tell me what's going on?'

'Some things just aren't worth explaining.' There was a warning in his eyes. *Don't go there.* His jaw tilted up. 'And it's your business because…?'

Apart from the fact her staff had apparently been dodging verbal bullets—oh, and the teensy-weensy fact that she'd shared his bed—she couldn't think of a single reason. Clearly he didn't attach any emotions to the other night and she needed to learn from that. Business as usual at the office. No time or space for emotions.

This one-night-stand thing was hard to get her head around. But if she was going to take charge of her life she had to get used to a lot of new things.

So she worked to keep it less personal. A pen lay on the top of a pile of files. She picked it up, twiddled it in her fingers, hoping it gave her more gravitas. 'Okay, well, here's an idea. You and Maitland Two could kiss and make up, at least at work. It would certainly stop us all having to duck for cover every time you meet.'

His eyebrows lifted, the message finally sinking into that messed-up brain of his. 'That bad, huh? No one's mentioned it before.'

'That's because you rule their world. Who would dare tell the marvellous Maitland twins off?'

'You?' For some reason that seemed to amuse him. 'Why doesn't that surprise me? You are quite surprising, you know. But you're probably right. It's been going on so long it's just the way we communicate. I guess it's just habit now.'

'Then go cold turkey, take a hypnosis course. Acupuncture? If you need help with the needles,

I'm a pretty good shot.' She jabbed the pen in his direction, sat back in her chair and fixed him with her best evil stare. 'I know exactly where to stick them for maximum pain…er, effect.'

He leaned across the desk until his mouth was inches from hers. Kissing distance. Inhaling distance. Goddamn, the desk would never be big enough. 'You certainly had maximum effect on me the other night, Nurse Radley.'

Heat shimmered between them. She caught her breath. It had all been going so well. She'd actually got him to see things from her point of view.

But now she just wanted to kiss him again. She looked at his mouth. The way his lips parted ever so slightly. They seemed to be infused with some kind of magnetic force that attracted her. Pulled her. Coaxed her forward. Inch by inch. Until the only thing she was aware of was the lightest whisper of his breath.

Oh, no.

She shifted her gaze. Over his perfect nose. Past some freckles she hadn't noticed before, dark, thick eyelashes. Up to his bright blue eyes. Saw the sparkle, the promise. The heat.

Bad move.

She swallowed and edged backwards out of immediate kissing range. 'Your nephew needs a solid loving family behind him.'

'And he has that. We all adore him. Surely you can see that everything we do, we do for Jamie?' His hand cupped her chin. 'You really care about him, don't you? What's that all about? What's it to you?'

How the hell had this shifted to being about her?

At his touch her breath hitched. She couldn't handle him touching her again, not here. Not ever. Didn't want the flash of need that he instilled in her, which she'd just about kept under control for ten days. The way he made her forget everything. Made her feel alive and hopeful.

But, God, he felt good. Smelt good. And she knew how great he tasted.

Smacking her lips together, she moved his hand from her chin and tried to focus on the conversation. 'I care about them all. That's why I took up paediatric nursing. They don't choose to get sick. They don't choose to grow up in a world that's fighting. Or have a say in how they're parented. Or by who.'

She sucked in air, trying to clear the tight knot that had lodged in her stomach. It wouldn't budge. And then it fused with the mish-mash of emotions

Max stirred up in her until she didn't know what she was doing. What she was saying. She tried to refocus. 'I want them all to have a nice life. Adults have too much to answer for.'

Before she realised it, he was on her side of the desk, standing over her, his hand in her hair. Fingertips stole their way up the back of her neck, into her ponytail. He tugged it loose. And she let him get away with it.

His mouth dipped to her ear. 'Your kids are going to have a great mum. A bit scary...but you'll be fighting their corner. That's good.'

He didn't mean anything by it. It was just a statement, but he'd hit a nerve. He made a habit of doing that one way and another. The man had a lot of annoying habits. 'What's that got to do with anything? I don't want kids. A family. I don't want any of that.'

'Oh, yes, I forgot. You don't want more. That right? You don't want commitment. You don't want more sex. And now you don't want kids. Life's just peachy as it is.' His eyes darkened for a second, his breathing coming fast and erratic. She could feel how turned on he was as he pushed against her. 'But you're wrong, Gabby. All women want more.'

'Well, I don't.' And she didn't. She really didn't.

But there was his mouth again. So close. A breath away.

Okay, the guy was a mind-reader. He was right, she did want more. More of him. More kissing. More lovemaking.

But that would get her damned to hell. 'No. I don't. Want. More.'

'Sure you do. Every part of you tells me so.' His hands fisted in her hair and he pulled her to him. For a second he stared at her with questions running through his eyes. He looked as confused as she felt. Weirded out by the wild rush of pure feral need.

But then his focus cleared and his mouth was pressing hard against hers. His tongue stroked her lips apart then dipped into her mouth, filling her with an ache, a heat that she'd never imagined was possible, and now never wanted to lose.

As he ground her against the desk she grasped his shoulders, rocked against him. Knowing that at any instant someone could barge into the office and find them. Knowing this was every kind of wrong. And dumb. And too risky.

But knowing that made her want him even more. It was like an illicit secret addiction that she had to feed. Each glance, each touch, stoked a need for the next fix. She moaned against him as he dragged her top up and palmed her breast through her bra.

She sighed with delight as he parted her legs and fitted his body between them. Through the thin fabric of her scrubs she felt the length of him, hot and hard. Scraping her nails down his back, she sat on the edge of the desk and wriggled against him.

His hot, wet mouth made her clamour for more kisses, his touch fired every nerve ending, every cell in her body into a frenzy of intensity. Putting all doubts aside, she writhed against him, and he ground back harder and faster. She heard gasps and moans, realising, with a shock, they came from her throat as he licked it.

And then, when she thought he just had to be inside her, somehow, condom or no condom, a release she wasn't expecting shuddered through her. He gripped her more tightly as she rubbed and rocked against his erection. Stilled as she let go. Finally let go. All the emotion and frustration and confusion, all the avoiding what was so totally obvious—that she wanted him with a passion that almost scared her—knotted into a tight, sharp fierce ball and exploded into a million pieces.

He held her gently and kissed her with tenderness as she came down from her high, smiled into her hair as she found her senses again. Stroked her head against his chest as she steadied her breathing.

Who the hell was this man who could satisfy her with just a touch?

Too soon he pulled away. Left her in her office, her mind a blur, her scrubs dishevelled and creased, the smell of him everywhere.

As he reached the door he turned and pierced her with a steely look. 'You do want more, Gabby. You just have to decide how much.'

CHAPTER FIVE

'HOW ARE THE FIRST few weeks going? Settled in okay?' Rachel, the senior staff nurse, put her glass of wine onto the pub table and squeezed into the empty seat between Gabby and Andrea, the ward clerk. Somehow they'd all convinced Gabby that the weekly ward night out at The Shed would help break the ice with the team.

And, secretly, she surmised, they'd try to find out what made her tick, where her soft centre was.

Which was why she was sticking to lemonade. She was all out of showing people her soft centre, especially people like Max. She'd shown him way more than she'd planned. Those mojitos had been the beginning of the ruin of her.

But having people to laugh and joke with without endlessly feeling she was being judged was like a breath of well-needed fresh Auckland air.

'If you mean have I managed to unpack yet, then no. There never seems to be enough time between shifts. Roll on my next day off.' When she'd probably still not be able to manage the gargantuan task of putting those heart-twisting boxes away. 'But I love the new place. The flatmates are great. And as for the job, it's everything I hoped it would be.'

'Great, yeah? There's a good vibe on that ward. Even better now you're there.'

'Thanks.' Heat rushed to Gabby's cheeks. Since that mind-blowing orgasm she'd barely been able to look at her desk without sinful thoughts. Which had had a seriously detrimental effect on her organisational management.

What had started as efficiency had puddled into just about satisfactory. She really did need to put Max out of her head. She was not kissing him again. Ever. 'I hope I've made things easier, but tell me if I get too bossy. It's my first charge nurse job and I don't want to blow it.'

'It was manic before, but you've organised us. We certainly needed it.' The woman's eyes lit up. 'I know, you should come on the ward trip to do the twilight kayak over to Rangitoto Island. It's in a few weeks. Put your name down. There's a list behind the nurses' station.'

'Ooh, I don't know. A kayak? Me?'

'Ah, you'll be fine. And if it's too much for you,

there's always a double kayak. I'm sure we could find a burly volunteer to paddle you across.' Rachel winked. 'Randy Roger the porter's always looking for opportunities.'

Gabby was well aware of Roger the porter's heat-seeking palms. Her backside had come into contact with them way too many times already. By accident, of course—so he'd assured her. 'I'm sure I'll manage.'

'It's great fun. We paddle over, have a picnic, then kayak back with lanterns as the sun sets. It's gorgeous. Think about it. We'd love you to come.'

Gabby got the impression Rachel was being genuinely friendly rather than trying to suck up to her. The heat from her cheeks settled into a general warm glow all round. It had been a great idea to move here. She wished she'd done it sooner. She was surrounded by warm-hearted, fun people who accepted her, seemed to like her. Regardless of her mother's taunts that had turned into the usual begging and manipulation, now down the telephone instead of in Gabby's face, this had been a very positive move.

Across the bar the door swung open and in strolled Max. The happy vibe Gabby had been relishing wobbled, spiked, dropped, then swirled around in her stomach for a few excruciating seconds.

She felt a sharp nudge in her ribs as Rachel did a mock swoon. 'He's got his name down for the kayak trip... Would that entice you?'

'Me? Max? No!' The words came out too sharply, too quickly. If Rachel muttered anything about 'protesting too much' she'd just about die.

It had been a one-off thing. That had morphed into a two-off thing. But it was still no big deal. Not anything to get worked up about, despite her heart doing a silly jig.

Her friend's eyebrows dipped. 'Come on. What's not to like? Those Maitland brothers make great eye candy. Double trouble and twice the fun. Especially Dr Make-You-Weep over there.'

Her colleague had been more than happy to share her inside information on Max in the past so Gabby tried to pump her for more. Doing a silent three Hail Marys for being so sneaky, she asked, 'So what's the deal between the twins?'

'Well, no one knows for sure because it all happened in Dunedin.' Rachel cupped her hand over her mouth and leaned into Gabby's ear. 'But apparently Max had a thing with Mitchell's girlfriend.

Word is, they haven't spoken a civil sentence to each other since.'

An affair? Max? With Jodi?

Now, that was interesting. Shocking. And would also explain the rift and the edge between Max and Jodi. But it didn't seem right. He might be a player and a charmer but Max wasn't the kind of man to do that. 'Are you sure?'

'Sure as eggs is eggs. Their lives are, oh, so complicated. None of us even knew Mitchell had a child until a few weeks ago. Strange, don't you think? There's a lot more to their story.'

'I don't believe it.'

'Don't believe what?' Max was leaning over her, the hint of a teasing grin fluttering over his lips.

Earth, swallow me up now. He had quintessentially bad timing. 'Oh…er…nothing. I mean…'

'Speechless isn't a word I'd usually associate with you, Nurse Radley.' Placing a glass on the table—a large glass, with a paper umbrella and lime squeezed onto the rim—he grinned. 'Your usual. Just the one. Wouldn't want you to get drunk, now. Don't know where that could lead.'

'Er…but…no…thanks. I don't…' And he damned well knew it. Knew she was here with her work colleagues. That she had no desire to be reminded about what had happened the last time she had been in here. With him. Drinking mo-bloody-jitos. And now to top off her mortification her words had got lost somewhere en route from her brain to her mouth. Judging by the wicked smile he gave her, he thought it was due to his hyped-up animal magnetism.

He was probably right.

His eyes locked with hers, glinting with mis-chief. 'Oh, go on. Have a sip. Taste it. Then you could give me a score…out of ten? For the drink… obviously.'

Before she could answer he'd taken everyone else's order and disappeared to the bar.

Rachel grabbed the glass. 'Well, if you don't want it, I'll do the honours.' She took a long gulp. 'Delish. And tell me, Gabby, how does Max Mait-land know what your usual is?'

From the heady heights of fun and relaxation things were rapidly going downhill. Gabby played the indifference card and shrugged. 'He probably asked the barman. I was in here a few weeks ago and tried the cocktails.' It wasn't technically a lie.

'Probably 'cos you're the charge nurse,' Rachel whispered, 'trying to get into your good books. Always good to have the boss on side.'

Trying to get into my... No. Do not go there. 'Yes, probably.'

'Or maybe you're in already...' Rach nudged her. 'You know what I mean? But be warned; he's broken a few hearts already, that guy. Won't commit. Maybe he's still in love with Mitchell's girlfriend.'

Gabby choked on her lemonade. 'I doubt it. On all accounts.'

Did he? Was he?

A small knot of anxiety tightened in her gut. She just couldn't imagine a scenario where Max would sleep with his brother's girlfriend.

If he knew the gossip machine wheels were greased by lies about his love life the man would be mortified. And worse... If they were true? Did she want to get involved with a man who'd do that to his brother?

Involved? Yeah, right. She was definitely getting ahead of herself.

Too soon he was back, edging into the gap Andrea had left. He slipped into the space, slipped into the conversation. Slipped far too easily back into the forefront of Gabby's focus.

She watched him laughing and joking with the others, the attention he gave the women. The jokey camaraderie with the guys. He dominated the conversation. The life and soul of the party. The centre of the group. All ideas bounced off him. All his comments were noted with due respect.

She watched the way he chatted with Rachel, her new knowledge in him tainting the way she read his behaviour. Charming, funny, attentive, but definitely not stepping over the line. Not like the other night when something had connected between him and her.

And hopefully he didn't kiss other charge nurses the way he'd kissed her the other day. Maybe he did. Maybe kissing charge nurses was his hobby. Others did motocross or tennis. He did kissing. Hell, he'd perfected the art.

Perhaps Mitchell had read too much into a flirty conversation between Max and Jodi. Perhaps… Oh, the whole scenario was making her brain hurt.

But asking him?

As if. How could she insist he didn't ask her questions and then break that very rule herself?

How she managed to get through the next two hours was beyond her. The more she focused on him, the more aware she became of the tiniest touch, the merest glance in her direction. The way he ran his hand through his hair when he talked about serious stuff. Or when his smile hit his eyes and she felt like the sun was shining.

Somehow she agreed to join the ward touch-rugby team. Stumbled through a conversation about the latest boy band to hit New Zealand. The best ski lodges for parties. The merits of beer versus spirits.

All the time trying not to inhale his scent. Trying not to react to the brush of his skin against hers. Ignoring the fire raging in her belly when he leaned back against her or when he glanced in her direction for her opinion on the dangers of snowboarding. When he caught her eye and gave her a cheeky wink or the heat of his palm on her thigh when he shifted to allow someone out of the group.

And the way that simmering tension between them seemed to grow exponentially until she felt she'd go mad if she didn't touch him. Run her finger down his cheek, through his hair. Press her lips against his.

Suddenly Rachel looked at the emptying table and checked her watch. 'Oh, goodness. Look at that, it's getting late. Got to dash. I'm on an early tomorrow. But it's been great. We should do this again.'

Gabby gathered her rapidly diminishing senses as she watched Rachel leave, realising that if she didn't go she'd be left alone with Max. 'Oh. Yes. I need to go home too.'

'You live in Boston Road, don't you?' Rach paused. 'I live round the corner from there—do you want to walk back with me?'

Did she? No. She wanted to lie in bed with Max Maitland. To stare out of his penthouse window at the sparkling harbour lights. Listen to his regular breathing as he slept with her in his arms.

But most of all she wanted him to make love to her. 'Yeah, okay, I'll come with you, Rach. Hang on a second, I'll just put my coat on.'

Max's hand on her wrist gave her pause. He turned her away from Rachel and hissed into her ear, his breath warm against her neck. 'Oh, no, you don't. Not so quick.'

'What? Why?' *Please don't touch me.* Her body remembered how he'd felt inside her. Every nerve ending screamed for his touch. Her nipples hardened as she brushed against him, her legs already weakened with desire. How could a man make her feel this alive? She had no idea how to deal with the stirred-up hormones racing through her system.

There was only one release, could only be one release. With him. But she couldn't go there again.

Vivid blue eyes fixed on hers, offering promises and chances, and a night of wicked pleasure. Hers for the taking.

'There's only one place you're going tonight, Charge Nurse Radley. And that's with me.'

'Don't think you can spend the whole evening flirting and teasing without some kind of comeback.' His hands were in her hair now as the lift sped them towards his apartment.

He brushed her curls back from her face and peered into those large, dark eyes that had such a strange hold over him. Running a thumb along her cheek, he watched her pupils dilate. They told him how much she wanted him, too. Again she wore a buttoned-up blouse that covered her skin. Again it was the sexiest thing he'd ever ached to remove from a woman's body.

All evening the only thing on his mind had been this moment. It had been inevitable from the first second he'd seen her in the bar.

He'd gone from determination not to act on his

impulses to trying to work out how the hell to get her alone again. And now, after all his promises to the contrary, they were headed back to the penthouse.

Pressing his lips against hers, he drank her in. This time he wanted to treasure the taste, learn everything about her, hear her moan, feel her shiver under his touch. He backed her up against the lift wall, his hands zoning in on those curves that kept him awake at night.

She pulled away, smiling. 'I wasn't flirting with you. I was chatting with friends. Rachel's going to think I'm a loony, sending her home in a cab while we… What was it you said? Talk about ward policies?'

'I was thinking on the hoof. You were driving me mad.'

'You think you're mad? Because I was trying not to think about you…us…this… I've signed up to kayak across an ocean, run myself ragged on a touch-rugby field and do a three-day cross-country skiing event. And I hate sport.' She laughed into his chest and he hauled her closer, feeling the press of her breasts against his diaphragm, inhaling the sweet scent of her shampoo. He'd never been so aware of a woman in his whole damned life.

'Really? I reckon you'd be good at anything you put your hand to.' He pulled her hand to his waist, ran his fingers over her bottom towards her thigh. 'With these gorgeous legs you'd excel at sport.'

'Oh, I used to. I was a pretty good athlete once, but it all…' Those pupils contracted. Heck, her whole body contracted. There was more to this but she'd clammed up. Turned away. 'Never mind.'

He grasped her wrist and turned her to face him, wishing there wasn't such a veil of secrecy over everything. Wishing trust wasn't something he'd heard about but never experienced. 'So what happened?'

The lift pinged and they were in his apartment before she answered. The vulnerability in her face tugged at his heart, raising more questions about her past. 'Life got in the way. You know how it is.'

'Do I?'

She wrapped her arms around his neck. Nibbled along his lip. 'Shut up and kiss me.'

He smacked a kiss on her mouth. Short. Hot. Hard. Pulled away before she got too comfortable. 'Stop avoiding my questions. You are allowed to talk just a bit.'

'Talking never achieved anything.'

'But it might help. This doesn't just have to be about sex.'

What? Since when had he encouraged a woman to talk? Since when had he wanted anything other than sex?

But Gabby—she was too many shades, too complex to get his head round. She wanted him to talk but refused to illuminate him on her past. She held back so far it was bordering on retrograde—but when she did let loose it was like setting off fireworks. He was caught firmly in her glare.

'Says the guy with commitment issues.' Frowning, she jabbed him in the ribs before walking through to the lounge.

He shrugged as he followed her. 'Commitment's overrated.'

'So I heard.'

'From whom?'

Her eyebrows rose. 'The hospital grapevine.'

'Again? We've been over this. You'll probably hear a whole lot of stuff. Doesn't make it true.'

'It was about Jodi and Mitch.' She paused, dark eyes scrutinising him.

God, it had to happen at some point. Now he felt like he was being put on trial. The truth serum was no doubt burning a hole in her pocket. Why the hell had he been encouraging her to talk? Kissing. Kissing's what mattered. Losing himself in her. Not relating a sad, sorry tale that benefited no one. He sucked in air. 'So what about Jodi and Mitch?'

'Well, actually, Jodi and you. Apparently you had a thing with her.'

'I did.' He didn't need the damned truth serum. Just one look from those eyes had him spilling the facts. Or at least as much as she needed to know. He had to wipe that dark look from her. Stat. 'But it was before Mitch ever got involved with her. Me and Jodi had a thing. Not a big thing but a thing.'

'A relationship thing? Serious?'

He winced. So that's where she was going, digging to see whether he was capable of caring. The bad news was he didn't believe he was. 'It's complicated. My whole damned life is complicated. Which boils down to the fact that I'm not good at relationships. I can't do it. Apparently I don't give enough, I'm too driven and I work too hard. Women don't like that.' He didn't even want to acknowledge why he did that, why he had to be the best at the cost of everything else.

But his uncle's endless stream of insults came

back to haunt him, along with the relentless competition to excel that marked both Maitlands as the top students through med school. The endless comparison that had been instilled into both of them from a young age. *Mitchell's got his driver's licence, you'd better pass yours. Make sure you get an A in maths—show Mitch how much better you are. Mitch doesn't want to see you at Christmas. He's too busy.*

The wedge that had been driven between them grew larger every year, until… 'After Jodi and I finished, Mitch asked her out.'

'Tacky.'

'Broke just about every rule as far as I was concerned. You don't date your brother's ex. Period. We were barely communicating as it was. But this just about finished us off.'

Similar to this conversation right now. Ignoring the barrier she'd thrown up between them, he stepped back into her space, wrapped a finger in one of her luscious curls and rested his forehead against hers. 'And that was a real passion-killer, right? I vote we forget about that stuff and rewind. Or fast forward or something.'

He also didn't want to admit how lately he'd ached to talk to Mitch. Just talk. Bridge that gap.

Making Jamie better had been a good step, but he didn't know how to take the next one.

Gabby stared up at him. 'Not yet. I'm not done.' Hell, she sure knew how to drive a hard bargain. 'So that's why you two are at each other's throats?'

'Yeah. Yes, it is.' She didn't need to know the rest of his ancient history. It was easier to finish it there.

She cupped his cheek and smiled, although there was still a slice of distrust simmering there in her eyes. But somehow she just knew when he was holding back. And somehow she knew when to stop needling him. 'Just so you know, I'm glad the rumours weren't true. I never thought you'd do something like that.'

'Good.' Finally. 'So where were we?'

Placing a finger to her lip, she thought. 'Commitment's bad, but talking is…?'

Clearly not a good idea. 'Oh, but there's all kinds of talking…' He kept his arms round her as he guided her to the kitchen in a kind of klutzy waltz, hoping to lighten the mood. Tightened his grip on her waist and swirled her round, then took the opportunity to kiss her again. 'There's sweet-talking.'

'Obviously you're good at that, otherwise I

wouldn't be here.' Her palms touched his chest as she giggled. A jolt of awareness surged through him.

If he didn't get her into bed soon he'd go mad, but if she needed convincing he could do that. He could do slow. He could wait. God knew, she was worth it.

He reached for the top button of her blouse and carefully undid it, then whispered into her neck, 'And there's shop talk… We really could discuss updating the policies.'

'Woo. Infection control has suddenly got very attractive.' She stepped back. 'But now you've just reminded me of another good reason why we shouldn't be doing this. Work.'

'I can think of lots of reasons why all of this could be really dumb, but can't say I'm focusing on those right now. Good God, woman. Let me kiss you.' Okay, so slow was killing him.

His lips brushed just behind her ear and he inhaled her sweet fragrance. Managed three more buttons. Just enough to reveal the lace of her bra and the creamy skin of her breasts. 'Extra-curricular bonding. That can only help team relations.'

'I don't know. It seems so wrong. Ooh.' Curling deeper into his arms, she gasped as he ran fingers over the lace cup of her bra. Her words and actions were out of sync. 'What if people find out? I don't want to be the subject of gossip, I've only just started there. I don't want my clean slate sullied.'

'Sullied? By me? I do not sully.' Reaching behind her, he unfastened the bra, skimmed his fingers over her skin and tweaked a nipple, enjoying the tight puckering at his touch. 'So we keep it to ourselves. Our secret. Seriously, no one needs to know.'

'I mean it. No one, not Mitchell or anyone.'

At the mention of his brother the familiar irritation rushed through him. He dropped his hand to his side. 'Like I'd tell him anything.'

'Don't you have some kind of spooky twin telepathy? Doesn't he know already?'

'Nah. But we do understand each other well enough to keep our distance.' His hand slid to her hip. 'Let's not talk about him. This...this is much more fun.'

She didn't look convinced. 'And we're both woefully bad at sharing things about ourselves.'

'But we're very good at making each other feel better about it. Neither of us wants to get involved.

When it's over, it's over. We walk away.' He ran his thumb over her swollen lips. 'No harm done.'

'No harm done. Really? You think that's likely?' She licked round the thumb tip, sending wild jolts of electricity through him. Then she sucked his thumb deep into her mouth. And out. And he felt powerless against this raging need zipping through him. 'We're consenting adults. We both know the score.'

She smiled hesitantly. 'So we do this? Bed buddies? Friends with benefits?'

'Can you stop it?'

She shook her head and stared at his chest, thought a while. 'I don't think so.'

'So we do it when we want to. Because we want to. As soon as we stop wanting to we call it quits. We may not want to spill our guts over our past lives, but we can at least be totally upfront about this. As soon as the spark dies, we're out.'

Tilting her chin up to him, he finally, *finally* held her gaze. Caught the need and the fire and knew it mirrored exactly what was in his eyes, too. But there was a glimmer of fear, too. Something that begged him not to hurt her. She was protecting herself. Had she been hurt before?

When her mouth opened he covered it again

before she could add to her damned list. Add to his own list.

And he promised her, with his kiss, that he wouldn't hurt her. Not if he could help it.

They didn't need a conversation, didn't need a mating dance. Didn't need anything to convince them they were headed straight to bed. They both knew it was as inevitable as night following day.

When he pulled away her breathing was ragged. Her eyes filled with that mist he'd seen the other day. The one that told him she needed him. Now.

'Which leads me nicely on to the best kind of talking…pillow talk.' He nuzzled against her throat as his fingertips ripped her blouse off and dropped her bra to the floor. Eyes feasting on her two perfect breasts, he felt the smile spread through his body. 'Would you look at that?'

'Oh.' She smiled and pretended to be surprised. 'Naked. How did that happen?'

'Not naked enough.' He gripped her hips and dragged her back to him, struggling with the need to have her now. On the kitchen floor. Against the bench.

Knowing that if he took her into his bed he wouldn't want her to leave. Would want to wake up with her tomorrow. And maybe the next day.

But not knowing how the hell to control this ache inside him. 'I know, let's have some champagne to seal our deal.'

'Are you trying to get me drunk? Just one small one.' Standing behind him, she peered over his shoulder. The fridge light lit up her face. No— her laughter lit up her face. 'Max Maitland, you have four bottles of champagne but no milk. No food…at all. What do you eat?'

'I eat at work.'

'That's it? Don't you cook?'

'No. I can cook—I just don't. We could phone out for takeaway. But in my book eating is cheating.' He popped open a bottle and poured bubbles into two long-stemmed glasses. Offering her one, he pointed towards the bedroom. 'Now, Nurse Radley, we have a lot of policies to work through… Shall we…?'

Her mouth formed a playful pout as she pretended to weigh up her options. Then she smiled, long and slow, and led the way. 'Hell, yes.'

CHAPTER SIX

'HOW COULD YOU?' Gabby tied Max's shirt-tails into a knot at her hip as her post-the-best-sex-of-her-life-times-three glow withered, just like the poor scrap of life she was looking at. Wilting and thirsty, the geranium's head hung limply in the weak early-morning sunlight. 'What the heck have you done to my plant?'

A bare-chested Max stepped onto the deck and handed her a cup of coffee. 'Yours, is it? I thought it was a present.'

'It's a present that now needs life support. You clearly can't look after it, so I claim part custody until you learn. It's *ours* then.'

'Okay. But you have to take charge of feeding time.' His arms snaked round her waist as he hugged her from behind. His heat wrapped around her like a cocoon. She leaned against him, unable to be angry after such an amazing night. He'd made sure she'd got exactly what she wanted, and when. And now she was hungry for more.

But still she was confused by the new turn of events. She had a bed buddy. It was the kind of thing other women did. People she read about, women she heard chatting in bars, sophisticated women, women who knew what they wanted and where they were going. Not grown women who, in their families' eyes, could never make up for a mistake committed over a decade ago.

And yet here she was. In a penthouse apartment with six feet three of sinful sex. Making up for a long time of celibacy.

Her nonna would be screaming a tirade of insults down from heaven. *Brazen. Sinful. Devil's child.*

She fought the instinct to put her fingers in her ears and block out the imaginary noise. Old Gabriella would have hung her head, like the plant, and withered and conformed to what was expected. New Gabriella laughed. 'We have something. That's a hoot.'

But as she peered more closely at the droopy leaves the laughter melted away. Nonna would be grinning along now. *Serves you right, wicked girl.* Again.

'Well, we did have something. Maybe it's a

sign.' Celestial retribution. She touched a leaf. It
came off in her hand.

Max grinned and stooped to pour his coffee
into the plant pot. 'I'm not good at these kinds of
things. I did warn you.'

'Wait! What are you doing? It needs water, not
a caffeine hit. What are you trying to do? Kill it
off completely?' She dashed inside to get a glass
of water and poured it over the wilting plant. 'And
it looks so lonely out here.'

'It's just a plant, for goodness' sake.'

'It's the beginnings of a garden, Max. And it
needs care and attention.'

'So do I.' He wrapped her in his arms and leaned
in for a kiss. 'Starting right now.'

Her back arched as she leaned away from him,
hands flat on his chest. The towel from after their
shower hung loosely at his hips. One false move…
one very good move…and he'd be naked. She
could already feel how hot she was making him.
How hard. 'Promise me you'll take more care of
it. Or no more kisses.'

'Na-ah. No promises.'

She shook her head. Wove her leg around his
and pressed her nipples against him. Gyrated her

hips in a dance of wanton desire. 'Promise, or no more of this.'

'Uh…huh.' At her insistence he nodded. 'Okay. Okay, I'll take more care of it. You are one crazy woman.'

'That's me. The crazy plant lady.'

'Maybe I like crazy plant ladies. Maybe you're my ideal woman.'

What happened to just friends with benefits? Her heart hammered in her chest. Ideal woman wasn't what she'd expected to hear. She'd been led astray before with that kind of comment and it had been the beginning of her downfall. So she'd learnt that lesson all too quickly. Never be charmed by a charmer.

But coming out of Max's mouth on such a beautiful morning, it felt like being caught in a ray of sunshine. 'How so?'

'Apart from that amazing thing you do with your finger…' He tapped her on the nose and guided her back towards the bedroom, his hand cupping her backside. 'You don't expect anything. You don't ask for anything. And you're pretty damned hot… God, I have so many things I want to do to you.'

'Ooh…' She turned into his arms, laughed at the

glint in his eyes. 'That sounds very, very promising. But I should be going.'

His warm breath stroked the nape of her neck. He unbuttoned the shirt, let her breasts fall free. Closed his eyes for a second and sighed. When he opened them again he gazed at her. First her face, then a long slow gaze down her body. 'My shirt has never looked so goddamned sexy. What do you say to taking it off and staying a bit longer? I have nothing planned all weekend except packing for a conference that suddenly seems deeply dull.'

'Oh? Where are you going?' Her teeth grazed the side of his neck as she arched against him. He hadn't mentioned anything about going away. It would happen, she supposed, as he was an eminent, internationally in-demand surgeon. She just hadn't expected the prospect of him not being around to feel so bleak.

'Singapore. Then a lecture tour in Malaysia.' His head dipped as he took a nipple into his mouth. Heat fizzed through her at every lick of his tongue. 'But what I really want is to stay here with you.'

'Gosh, the life of a surgeon is so glamorous.' She tugged playfully on the fold of towel at his waist, hoping to make the most of the time they had left. 'How long will you be away?'

'Too long. But you're not back at work until Monday, so how about we spend the next twenty-four hours in bed?'

'God, yes.' She couldn't help the moan escaping from her lips. He had a way of driving her mad with one touch. One look. But her stomach growled, reminding her she hadn't eaten for a long time. 'But at some point we really do need breakfast. I need to replace some of that well-spent energy.'

'Later… I'll phone out later. I have other plans for my mouth right now.' His lips were on her breast, sending arcs of need spiralling through her. He edged her back onto the bed, kissed a trail down her ribs.

Suddenly, uninvited and unwanted, a shrill, silly pop tune stalled them.

Max's phone.

Already anticipating much more of what they'd spent the best part of the night doing, Gabby placed her hand on his arm. 'Don't answer it.'

'I have to.'

She groaned. 'It's your day off.'

'I don't get those.' He slid out of her grip, snatched the phone and frowned. 'Maitland.'

For a second he said nothing. Nodded. His breathing sped up, his jaw tightened. But his voice was soft and warm. 'Oh, hi. No, it's fine. Fire away...' He covered the phone speaker with his hand and turned to Gabby. 'It's Jodi.'

Then he tightened the towel round his waist, turned his back on her and left the room, resuming the conversation with his ex-girlfriend-turned-girlfriend-in-law. 'Yes, that's right. Thirty milligrams, three times a day. But if you hang on I'll come in now to check. I'll be there in five. No...you're not interrupting anything...nothing important.'

'Oh.' *Nothing important.* Again? Had she not learnt her lesson? Shivering in the now-cold room, Gabby sat up and wrapped the duvet round her. A tight fist of disappointment lodged in her chest. 'Oh. Okay. That's how it is. Well, I was going anyway.'

Although she knew he hadn't meant it quite the way it had sounded, she suddenly felt like a spare part. A tiny piece in Max's busy life. Insignificant. He'd told her it was over between Jodi and him, and she was just the mother of one of his patients. His brother's girlfriend.

But it all seemed so intensely complicated. The brothers. Their rift that set the whole hospital on edge at times. This. Here.

Keeping everything on a need-to-know, ask-no-questions basis was all well and good, but it meant there was little connection. Nothing real. And the realisation that she wanted either something real or nothing at all hit Gabby hard.

And she definitely wanted to be something important.

Clearly bed buddies wasn't her thing after all. Who was she trying to kid? Fun, sure. But the flip side to fun was expendable. Superfluous. Not needed.

She didn't want to be picked up and dropped when it suited. Didn't want to be the one doing that either. Because they'd agreed on equal terms, so she could do the dropping too.

For goodness' sake. He'd just spent the last few hours caressing her, whispering to her, sleeping with his arms round her, refusing to let her go. They'd even dispensed with condoms, using her pill as contraception—so as to get the deeper connection, skin on skin.

But however connected they were physically, they'd never be connected emotionally. Not when either of them refused to give.

Putting her feet firmly on the floor, she gathered her wits. These weird displacement feelings were a shock.

She needed to get out. She needed to be sure of what she wanted. And that certainly wasn't to be a spare part.

As soon as the spark dies...

That didn't look like it would happen anytime soon. If anything it was getting more intense—at least for her. She was learning fast that Max was the kind of guy she didn't want to pick up and drop at will. The kind that she wanted to stay with way longer than was good for her, after the sex and the sleeping.

She needed to get out before the spark ignited and she got too caught up in the flashback.

As she got dressed to the sound of his laughter bubbling through from the lounge, a hot sting burned at the backs of her eyes. A love life was something she hadn't allowed herself to think of for ten years. *Ten years.* Doing penance for a mistake she would never repeat. And never truly recover from. So this was so not the time to discover she wanted the whole damned package and more. And with Mr I'm Sexy, who wouldn't know commitment if it walloped him in that too-damned-pretty face. Not a chance.

He was still talking as she disappeared once again from his apartment when he wasn't looking. Hitting the city street, she hauled fresh air into her lungs.

And renewed her determination to never again lose control of her life and her heart.

'I'm so grateful you've come.' Jodi's smile wavered as Max neared the cubicle. Even though her eyes were ringed with shadows and her hair wasn't as tidy as she liked to keep it, she was still breathtakingly beautiful.

Just an objective observation.

He checked his heart. No—no feelings there, except genuine concern for her and his nephew. And a little sadness, perhaps, that things had ended the way they had with Jodi. She'd been one in a string of women who'd berated him for his dedication to work and unwillingness to commit. They'd had fun, though, before they'd broken up. At least, he had.

Apart from being his brother's girlfriend, she was nothing to him now.

And yet when Mitchell had announced—no, bragged—that he was seeing her, their animosity had thickened. Years of frustration, hurt and lack of contact melded into a fierce rivalry.

Then, after she'd turned up with a child who was unmistakably a Maitland, he'd had a mixture of feelings. Jealousy had been centre stage, although he hadn't been able to see it at the time. Anger, he'd thought, at a brother's bond being broken.

But now he had to wonder—jealous about what? The fact Mitchell had Jodi again? Or that he had a ready-made family? That, despite how sick Jamie was, Mitchell had found love and happiness?

And he himself had found what? A fulfilling career, sure. But there was little fulfilling about the rest of his life. Did he want kids? That thought whacked him square in the gut. Hell, he didn't know. Hadn't contemplated it until Jamie had come on the scene.

But today all he felt was just eagerness to help them get sorted out. Then he could get back home.

Amazing what hot sex with a prim, buttoned-up charge nurse could cure. He kept his smile in check. Finally he'd found someone just like him—wanting nothing more than a good time, even if she'd done her disappearing act again. One of these days, maybe, he'd actually wave her off or even accompany her out of his apartment, instead of turning round and finding she'd done a bunk. Again.

And it was no end of irritating to realise he missed her again, too. Somehow she'd grown on him in unexpected ways. She'd probably just popped out to get breakfast.

But, goddamn the woman, couldn't she have left a note?

He closed the cubicle curtain around the bed to create a little privacy, trying to focus on the matter in hand. 'So what's the problem, Jodi? The meds dosage is being titrated so it's going to be different on different days until he stabilises…but you sounded panicked on the phone. Something else bothering you?'

'I overheard one of the nurses say that a couple of the kids here had gone down with some sort of vomiting bug. I need to get Jamie off this ward now.'

Great. That's all they needed: a compromised child and a virulent gastro bug. 'Yeah, the anti-rejection drugs do silly things with Jamie's immune system. He'll be vulnerable.'

'You're the only one with authority to discharge him. Mitchell said he'd sign a self-discharge form if you…disagreed.'

'I won't. Why would I?'

She paused. 'Oh, I don't know…'

'In case I was difficult? Right?' Max pulled at his shirt collar. Something was irritating him, but he couldn't tell whether it was outside his body or more than skin deep. He shrugged. Checked the charts. 'Jamie's doing fine. I'm still a little concerned about getting all the dosages right, but I agree he'd be better off at home than at risk here. You can bring him in to Outpatients and we'll take it from there.'

'You hear that, baby? We're going home,' she whispered to Jamie, her voice thick with tears. 'I didn't think this day would ever come.'

The little guy jumped up and down on the bed—thrusting an old fire engine into Max's hand, those brilliant blue eyes blazing with mischief.

Suddenly an image popped into Max's head of him and Mitchell—not much older than Jamie—in some sort of den they'd constructed with a clothes airer and a sheet in their old house. The

one they'd been dragged away from in such a
hurry that fateful night.

Under the sheet they'd been laughing about a
shared joke, chatting in twin-speak, the strange
gobbledegook language they'd made up. He'd forgotten. Forgotten they'd once had such a strong
bond that no one else had even understood them.
Just the two of them, inseparable. Emotion clogged
his throat and he sucked in air.

So many things he'd blocked out in order to
cope. Easier to push everything—everyone—
away than risk emotional overload. Easier to forget than to drag everyone down with him.

Their mother's face had been a mix of emotions as she'd popped her head under the sheet
and laughed in confusion. 'You two, what a pair!
You're always up to something. Would you one
day let someone else into your private jokes?'

The memory was infused with the pungent
smell of flowers. Was that her perfume? No...
He tugged at the memory to try make it more
real, but the more he tugged the harder it was
to grasp. It disappeared into a mist, leaving him
heavy-hearted and face to face with a red fire engine and a toothy smile. 'Max...play.'

Taking the fire engine out of her son's hands,

Jodi ran it along the bed frame. 'I don't think Uncle Max has time to play, right?'

It was an invitation to leave. He was torn. He wanted to sit here and play with his brother's son for a few more minutes. Be a part of their lives. But he didn't know if Mitchell would take kindly to that. Instead, he had to let them all go. The irritation seemed to thicken the back of his throat now, his words struggling to come out. 'No, 'fraid not, buddy. Uncle Max has to go. But I'll see you…'

Jodi nodded. 'At Outpatients.'

'Yes.' He turned to go, but realised he needed to say something more. 'I'm really sorry for how everything has turned out.'

She gave him a shy smile. 'You mean you and me? Or you and Mitch?'

'I should have treated you better. But I'm glad you're with Mitch now. You both seem happy.'

'We are. He's not that bad, you know.' She winked.

'That's what they said about Attila the Hun.' When she laughed again he joined in and it felt great. Strange, but great, to have made some inroads.

Gabby was right. Maybe he and Mitch should

call a truce—he just didn't know how to take that step. Maybe have that beer in The Shed, and a chat. Would his brother be open to that? A chat? That was something they hadn't managed for a long time. Seemed Gabby was right about way too much for her own good.

Jodi patted his arm and smiled. 'I can't thank you enough for what you've done. Perhaps you could come round to the house sometime? See how things go? Jamie would like that.'

'And Mitchell?'

'Give him time. I'll work on it.'

'Okay. Yes. I'd like that. If it's not too much trouble.' He slipped a kiss on the boy's head and huffed out a breath. Things were starting to look up, a chance at making something better with Mitchell, being part of Jamie's life. And a damned fine night spent with a gorgeous woman—with promises of a whole lot more. Her plans for a truce were finally taking form. He couldn't wait to tell her he'd actually been invited to his brother's house.

Now all he had to do was find her again.

Hours later he sloped back to his apartment block, tired, hungry and distinctly annoyed. Not knowing the correct address of the woman he was sleeping with was an error he wouldn't make again. He'd hammered on half the doors in Boston Road. Hadn't clicked at first that it was a damned main road that stretched for miles. And why the hell did she have her phone switched off? She had hours before she was back on duty, and that meant hours to play.

Turning the corner towards his front door, he was semi-blinded by a riot of colour. And now irritation almost burst out of him. Damn. He didn't want her silly gifts, he wanted her. Now. In bed.

But she'd sneaked back when he'd been out and had brought him a trio of ghastly plants identical to the last one. Okay, not identical. These at least looked alive.

Three—the same number of times they'd made love. Ah, the reality started to sink in.

Plus, she'd left a basket of oranges, pineapple, bread and milk. A tub of plant food. This time there was no note. He checked. And checked again, his good mood rapidly degenerating.

Shoving the door open and backing into his flat with his arms overflowing, he finally nailed what was bugging him. This wasn't a thank-you gift.

Or a friendly gesture. It wasn't an *I'll be back soon to share.*

It was a kiss-off. A goodbye.

CHAPTER SEVEN

Six weeks later...

'AND THAT, MY FRIENDS, is a wrap,' Max raised his voice above the upbeat rock music that accompanied every closure he did. As he finished securing the final clip on his patient's swollen belly, the usual wave of relief hit him in the gut. It was only the beginning of a long journey, but at least the old guy had a chance now. 'I'll check on him when he's out of Recovery. Any problems, call me. I'll be up in the paediatric HDU.'

'HDU? Why? We don't have a patient there at the moment, do we?'

Deflecting the strange looks from his registrar, Max lobbed his gloves into the pedal bin, flicked off his surgical gown and washed his hands. 'I think I left my keys up there. Just going to check.'

'I could phone up if you like. Save you the trouble.'

Goddamn, could the man not leave him alone? 'No worries. I could do with the exercise.'

Surgery couldn't go fast enough these days. Not when his body had a homing instinct straight to the HDU.

Turning the corner, he saw Gabby leaving the staff cafeteria, coffee in hand. He jogged to catch her up and fell into step. 'I was just on my way to find you. In your usual hurry again, Nurse Radley?'

She offered him a wobbly smile, hesitant and unsure. Despite the confident outward appearance she liked to show the world, he could read every emotion flitting across her eyes. Today it was embarrassment, uncertainty and a dash of heat.

It wasn't that she didn't want him, then. Even after all this time her cheeks still heated at the sight of him. It was that she'd decided she couldn't, for some reason. 'I'm trying to get back to the ward. Since that gastro bug hit the hospital we've been rushed off our feet and painfully short-staffed. It took everyone out in waves.'

'But we haven't spoken properly for weeks.' And since the moment he'd walked back into his bedroom and found her gone, again, he'd had a keen sense of loss. Something missing from his life. Something missing from his bed. Now he finally had her attention he was going to keep it. 'I liked the way we were before. When we had a laugh.'

'You're very busy and important, Max. You went away to a conference for a fortnight—can't blame me for that—and I couldn't help getting sick. You've seen me most other days.'

'And every time I hit your radar you disappear behind a curtain with a patient or into a meeting. The toilet. Lunch. Timbuktu. It's close on six weeks since...' Okay, so, yes, he'd been counting. No big deal. He just, well, he missed her.

Dating other women had been dropped from his agenda, as had mindless sex. Nothing seemed quite as vibrant and bright without her in it—particularly his apartment, although his deck was all kinds of Technicolor with those darned flowers.

Putting his hand on her arm, he managed to get her to focus on him. Stopped himself from planting a kiss on those chocolate-stained lips. 'Look, we need to talk.'

Uncertainty flickered behind her eyes. 'We do? Why?'

'I have news.' His chest swelled. He'd been trying to tell her this for days. It was ridiculous to be so damned excited about something so inane.

Her lips tightened. 'What do you mean? News?'

'We're going to be parents.'

'What? What on earth are you talking about?' Her cheeks pinkened, her eyes narrowed. For a second she looked spooked—no, abjectly terrified. She shook her head. 'No...no, we're not. We can't—'

'Yes. One of the plants has a new sprout. I think it's having a baby.'

'Really? The plant?' To his relief her mouth relaxed and she laughed, running her fingers over that silver heart at her throat. 'I thought you meant... How could you...? Oh, never mind. Wow. You've done good.'

He nodded. 'I know. And thank you, by the way, for the three extra mouths to feed. Now that I have a jungle family to care for, I don't have time to sleep.'

'The geranium needed company. And seeing that champagne isn't classed as an essential food group, I thought you needed some decent nutrition in your fridge, too. It was the least I could do.' And she truly did look a little shame-faced that she'd sneaked out on him again.

'Especially after you vanished, leaving me hard and half-naked and wanting you so much I thought I was going to die.' Ignoring her frown, he steered her to the laundry loading bay. Luckily it was deserted, save for a very large truck. He pulled her behind it, out of sight from the main corridor. 'Thing is, I had a lot more in mind that day.'

Holding her coffee cup up as a barrier, she tugged away from him. 'Well, I considered what you had to do—whatever that was—a lot more *important* than what we had planned.'

Was he missing something here? She was making a point but it was beyond him. 'I had to go and sort out Jamie's discharge meds. Then there was that conference. I did come and look for you.'

'I know. I understand.' But she wasn't giving him much hope for any sort of reconciliation.

'We miss you.' At her frown he explained. 'Our family.'

'You are so ridiculous.' She started to walk away, chucked her coffee cup into the trash, along with his hope. The conversation ended.

He reached out for her, but she was too quick. 'Wait, Gabby.'

His phone rang. 'Wait…'

Her back stiff, she retreated into the main corridor. 'Busy day, Mr Maitland.'

Now they were back to 'Mr' again. 'Wait.'

In three strides he caught her up, grabbed her hand. His phone blared again.

She tugged.

His phone screeched louder. 'Oh…crap.' He lifted the phone to his ear. 'Maitland.'

She stopped. Waited for him to finish his conversation. The whole time she stared at him, unable to wriggle out of his grip. Her face darkened, reddened, lips tightening into the thinnest line he'd ever seen. Her eyes blazed raw and black. And all he could think of was how she'd looked sprawled on her desk, panting and spent. Vulnerable, but so vibrant. How he wanted to make her wriggle like that again.

He flicked his phone back into his pocket. 'Your desk is only two floors away. We could make it in five minutes. Two if we run. What do you say?'

'I say let go of me, Maitland, or I call Security.' Her voice was loud and unwavering.

Smiling as sweetly as he could, he leaned into that soft, sweet-smelling spot at the nape of her neck. 'Okay, we're at work, and it doesn't feel right, that's fine. But listen, I have a kidney on its way from Dargaville. And a recipient driving up from Cambridge. I have to operate. Today. Or both the kidney and the patient will die. But I will be free after that.'

'So?'

'So you are six hours away from the best sex of your life. Do not walk away from me now.'

'You have no respect.' Pinching his hand with her free fingernails, she sent jarring spiky pains through his skin.

'Ouch. What the…?'

Grabbing his moment of weakness as an opportunity, she wrenched her fingers out of his. Shoved her fists on her hips and looked at him the way his uncle used to. A long time ago, but he still felt that familiar sting of shame, usually two seconds before he'd felt the sting of the belt. He was expecting the *must try harder* retort. He'd clearly disappointed her and he didn't know why.

She scowled at him. 'You don't want a relationship, Max. That I can understand. You don't want to commit. I get that too, I really do.'

'So what's your problem?'

'*Your* problem is I will not be left waiting naked in bed…only to hear you describe me as "nothing important".'

He would have reached out to her again but valued his intact skin too much. 'You thought I meant you?'

'You *did* mean me. Us. Spending the day in bed.'

'I didn't mean it like that. It was a slip of the tongue.'

'It came out all too easily, Max. And as I lay there naked and waiting, I got to thinking. I thought I was happy with our arrangement. It was fun, it sounded like a good idea. All grown up and sassy.' Her shoulders slumped forward a little and her voice got smaller. 'But I've never done anything like that before. I'm just not cut out to have sex and walk away.'

'You managed it quite well before.'

Her eyes blazed. 'But don't you see? I didn't manage it at all. It was a mistake. I thought it was the kind of sophisticated Auckland thing to do. I thought I could walk away unscathed, but I can't. I can't treat you like that and I definitely deserve more respect. I'm not a toy and I'm not going to be treated as *nothing*.'

'Whoa. I didn't realize. I messed up pretty big, didn't I?' He'd blown it. Acted like a jerk, trying too hard to please Jodi, look after Jamie, rise in his brother's unforgiving eyes. And had hurt her in the process. Not realised that, despite her bravado, in reality Gabby needed more from him. Trouble was, he didn't know if he was capable of giving it. 'I'm sorry, Gabby.'

'Yes, me too. But it wasn't working.'

He'd heard those words before. Too many times. And each time he'd thought it was someone else's problem. Not his.

But maybe she had a point. A small one. And worse, this time he didn't want to lose this thing they had. Sure, he was going soppy in his old age, but he liked having her around. Hell, he ached to have her around. He wanted to fall asleep with her, wake up with her again. He liked the way she added colour to his apartment. She just needed to be convinced. 'We can fix this.'

'I don't think so, Max. Not by taking me to bed again or having a quickie over my office desk. That won't work.'

'Then what would?'

She stalked away, her words trailing back to him on a hiss. 'Hell, if you can't work it out with all those fancy medical qualifications, you are six hours away from *missing* the best sex of your life.'

Atta girl. He smiled as he watched her retreat.

He was not going to miss out on that sex for anything. Challenge was his middle name. And that was the kind of gauntlet he could run.

Six hours, three minutes and fourteen seconds later, Gabby carefully placed the last of her blue boxes into the bottom of her wardrobe with a heavy heart and dashed to answer the door.

'You're late,' she said, to the thick green spiky bush bristling outside on her porch. She wouldn't admit to the ridiculous rabble of butterflies flexing their wings in her stomach.

But… What. The. Hell? He'd actually thought about what she'd said. That he'd even turned up was an amazing step forward. That he'd come with a plant rocketed him to idol level.

It was scary, but it was a start. Her emotions hovered between *let's get back between the sheets* and *run for the hills*. For well over a month she'd kept a lid on her emotions, thought she'd conquered her weakness for irritating transplant surgeons. When she'd lobbed those words at him earlier she'd believed there wasn't a chance in hell he'd actually rise to the bait.

She should have known better. He was a Maitland, after all—they always played to win. 'And you have to go one better, don't you? A small plant would have sufficed. A bunch of flowers? Chocolates?'

The bush wobbled as branches edged their way through the door. 'Give me a break, will you? Walking a tree down the road is harder than you think. And it's got teeth.'

'It's a cordyline *bush*, not a tree, and, no, it hasn't.'

He laughed. 'You know way too much about plants and all that.'

How could she take a talking cordyline seriously? 'I was brought up on a lifestyle block. We did outdoorsy things.' Too many. Then stuff had happened. Isaac had happened. And now she had to live with the fallout. They all did.

Sucking in a big breath, she closed that door in her mind. Some decisions she'd have to live with, but she was determined to move on. She'd been destined for great things, her nonna had said— so Gabby was going to make sure they happened. 'Come on, let's take it through to the garden.'

Max stopped short as he squeezed out the back door. 'Garden? Garden? This is worse than mine.'

'I'm working on it. The landlord has the audacity to describe it as an oasis. But, look, I have herbs and a flower bed.' Kicking the dry earth, she sighed. 'It's very different from the soil in Wellington.'

'Okay, so you're from Wellington.' His words were muffled slightly by foliage.

'Yes. Well, we live in a small township just north.' They truly knew little about each other yet had been so intimate. Talking to him now, without the pressure of work or sex, was easy. Her words just tumbled out, unguarded. She'd have to be careful of that. 'It's a farming community with people trying to scratch out a living. We have a few hectares.'

Land that had depended on her being there to help tend it in what little spare time she'd had. God knew what state it was in now. Her mother would have to cope without her. That would be a first. 'There were only three of us—Mum, my grandmother and me—so I had to help out a lot around my studies and work. We sold our produce at the local farmers' markets.'

'Sounds fun.'

'Sounds stifling.' With her dominating grand-mother and manipulating mother, it sounded very much like the prison it had become.

A dull ache squeezed in her abdomen and she

ran her hand over her belly as a wave of nausea rippled through her. Memories affected her in too many ways these days.

'Not a lot of fun, then?'

She breathed away the pain. 'Hardly living life on the edge, no.'

Late-afternoon sun filled the dusty courtyard, giving the place a feeling of summer, although they were far from that. But the sunshine warmed her, gave her a sense of optimism. She was here in Auckland with a fabulous job and a gorgeous man.

Gabby leaned against the doorframe, watching Max bend to put the plant on the ground. Maybe she could get over her anxieties about spending time with him, maybe they could work on the friends thing. That would be nice. She'd been working so hard she'd barely had time to make friends. Maybe…just maybe the benefits could come later. Once she'd got her head around her emotions.

But watching him straighten up and turn to face her, his eyes squinting in the sun, hair mussed up from plant-carrying, her breath was stripped from her lungs. God, he was gorgeous. Getting her head around her emotions might take a little time. 'So, you came here for...? A reason? Surely not just to bring gifts?'

He stepped forward, his mouth curling into a smile. 'I came to apologise. Seems to me we've gone about this all the wrong way: sex first then trying to learn about each other afterwards.'

'Isn't that your mojo? You should be used to it, surely?'

'Kind of. But I really do think we should clear the air. Let's go out.'

Her heart began to hammer against her ribcage. She was scared that the more she learnt about him, the more she'd like. And then the harder it would be to let go. And she didn't want this to be a sympathy invitation either. Or just another of his games. Because she knew he liked to win and she wasn't sure she was up to fighting him. 'Are you asking me out on a date? Because I don't think so.'

'No. Not a date. It's a getting-to-know-you... meeting.' He grinned. 'And as you're newish to Auckland I thought I'd take you sightseeing.'

'And what about our commitment issues?'

His eyes widened in surprise. 'Whoa. Straight talking as always, Nurse Radley. It's a dinner invitation, not a marriage proposal. The issues still stand. But I thought you might consider overlooking them, at least for tonight.' He stuck out his hand; it was warm and firm as she fitted hers into it. 'Gabby, please do me the honour of accompanying me for the evening. If we have fun, we may consider repeating it again tomorrow. Much more than that, I don't know.'

'Well, I've never been asked out on a non-date with a guy who can't plan past tomorrow before. This could be interesting.' Everything about his words and what she knew about him should have sounded alarm bells. But how could she turn down a plant-bearing sex god who just wanted to clear the air? 'I'll get my shoes.'

She dropped his hand and dashed inside the house, aware of his eyes on her the whole time. Question was, could she get in and out of her bedroom without him actually glimpsing her space?

'Or we could just skip the dinner thing.' He leaned lazily on the doorjamb, the heat in his eyes stoking the charge in her stomach. 'After all, one thing I can do is give you a good time. But you know that already. This your room?'

'No! Don't come in here.' *No. No.* Her heart thumped loudly as she shook her head. She couldn't have him in her room. Not until she was certain everything had been unpacked into its correct place. Until there was no way he'd see her things and think she was more crazy than she actually was.

He kicked the door open gently with his toe. Then frowned at the neat and tidy space. 'What's wrong, are you hiding a dead body or something?'

'No. It's just personal.' *Ask no questions, I'll tell you no lies.*

'Hey, it was a joke.'

'Oh. Sorry.' Seemed she'd overreacted. But how could she explain the things she kept in there without breaking her heart all over again? She had to get him out and do some air-clearing herself. 'So, let's go. Where are we headed?'

The questions in his eyes faded a little as his smile found its place again. 'First stop, the Sky Tower... You did say you were okay with heights?'

'This was not what I thought you meant.' Gabby's heart jumped and skittered as she stood dressed in a deeply unflattering blue and yellow jumpsuit and clutching a large metal clip attached to a harness. The windchill at one hundred and ninety-two metres was surprising, and it whipped her voice away a little. Either that or she truly was scared out of her wits.

Okay, yes. She was truly scared out of her wits.

She had to shout to make herself heard, but knew Max wasn't listening anyway. He had that determined look on his face that told her the man wasn't for moving. 'I thought we were having dinner here in that fancy revolving restaurant I've heard so much about. I prefer being inside. I prefer eating. Can we go back in? Please?'

Smiling, he adjusted her harness. 'Come on, fearless Gabby isn't scared? Surely not. Time to live life on the edge. Didn't you say you hadn't had a lot of that?'

'Is being up the top of this thing not enough? Now you want me to jump off it, too?'

'It's not dangerous. You're held on by a wire. Not like real base jumping. This is tame.' He brushed back a wayward curl that had blown into her face by the sky-scraping hurricane. 'I will if you will.'

'It's still a long way down at eighty-five kilometres an hour.' Yes, she'd listened to the instructions, read the notices, memorised the safety routine. If she was going to jump to her death then she would be well informed doing it. She curled into the heat of his palm, hoping he'd cup her cheek and kiss her. Then she'd find the strength to do this. 'I'll only do it if I can push you off first. You deserve nothing less.'

Damn right she had enough strength to do that.

'Deal.' He gave Jason, the jump master, the thumbs up. 'Ready when you are, boss.'

But Gabby held on tight to the rail. She peered over the edge to the streets below, where antlike people went about their normal lives rather than self inducing heart attacks at the top of the tallest tower in the southern hemisphere. Oh, and the building was swaying too. Great.

Then she slowly lifted her head and gazed out across the panorama of the city buildings and further still to the ocean. Another cruise ship was docking—it seemed tiny from this height. 'But why? Why this?'

'Two reasons. Firstly, it's a rite of passage. You can't come to Auckland and not do this.'

'You want to bet? I'm sure there's plenty of people who have never done this. I want to be one of them. I like never having done this.' The wind whipped up harder now, making the platform shake. The noise of the rattling metal echoed her erratic heartbeat.

'Then they haven't lived.' His hand covered hers and squeezed. 'And, secondly, it's about trust.'

'Now I'm really confused.' She'd started to shiver.

Putting his arms around her, he drew her close. She hesitated slightly, but he nodded and she went willingly into his embrace—as far as the wires and the harness and the clips allowed.

There was something so protective about him— his regular breathing, the heat of his body, the way he held on to her as if he'd never let her go. Ironic, then, that he wanted her to jump into nothing, supported by a flimsy wire. He whispered into her hair, 'Would I do anything to hurt you?'

He'd already hurt her once with careless words. 'I don't know.'

'Okay, not quite the answer I was hoping for.' He blinked. 'Do you trust me?'

'No.' That she did know, categorically. How could she trust a man who said she was nothing? But, then, at least he was trying to make up for it. In a spectacularly lofty way.

'Do you want to start trying?'

'It's too hard.' She wanted to believe he wouldn't hurt her. But she'd been there before—trusted a man—and it had ended in way more than tears.

He tipped her chin up and gazed at her. 'Trust me on this, Gabby. This is the best fun you'll have in years. You won't believe you found the courage to do it, but I know you'll ace it.'

Jason tapped his watch. The sun had started to dip below the horizon and if they were going to get the most out of this they'd have to do it now.

She watched Max edge to the front of the deck. There was little now between him and the ground, many, many metres below. The closer he got to the edge the more her stomach felt like it was dropping.

As he stood with his toes hanging over the edge of the thin platform, her heart rate went into overdrive, her legs barely held her up. He craned his neck round and winked. 'You can do this, Nurse Radley.'

This was exciting. Life-affirming. She shuffled forward, caught an intake of breath as she pressed her palms on his back. Caught her own scream as she forced all her frustration, her fear, her anger, her excitement…her growing need for him into her hands.

And pushed. 'See you at the bottom, Maitland.'

Then he disappeared into the air and for a second she thought of all the bad things that might happen. But that wouldn't. That this was indeed about trust. He wanted her to let go.

He'd brought her here to do this because it wasn't just an epic adventure, it was something fun they could share. A platform on which to base a friendship. *Do you remember that time you pushed me off the Sky Tower? I remember your screams as you flew.*

A platform for trust. A beginning.

Slowly, slowly.

Then it was her turn.

God. It was such a long way down. Such a leap of faith; in the wires and technology, in Max. In herself. Her courage almost failed her. She couldn't do this, didn't have the guts. She didn't.

So, she could remove the harness and go back inside to safety, or she could embrace this danger. She could turn it into a line, a line drawn between what had gone before and whatever happened next.

Old Gabby would never have done this. Old Gabby would never have been allowed to step out on here and risk her life, risk anything. But new Gabby—well, she could do anything she liked.

You do want more, Gabby, Max had said. And he was right. She did. She wanted fun and excitement, friendship, a rewarding job. The things everyone hoped for, that she'd been denied too long. Most of all, she wanted him.

Looking at the tiny shapes below, she wished she'd gone first, wished that the last thing she'd seen had been Max's face, felt his mouth against hers. She could just about make him out down there, standing away from the big red X, his arms outstretched as if to catch her. Would he? Was she putting her faith in too much? How messy would it be when it ended? Because surely nothing this amazing would last.

Gripping the rail with both hands, she hesitated. She did have a choice. She just had to make it. Could she take a chance? Dare she?

She imagined him calling her name.

Then she let go and jumped.

CHAPTER EIGHT

'OH. MY. GOD. Oh. My. God. I don't believe I did that.'

'Good, eh? I told you it was fun.' Max laughed at Gabby's wide eyes and pink cheeks. She hadn't stopped cursing and squealing since they'd unhooked her. And the fact he'd put that smile there fed his satisfaction no end. 'Rate it for me?'

Her grin spread. 'Five hundred and fifty thousand out of ten. Can we do it again?'

'Oh, no, I've unleashed an adrenalin junkie.' He shook his head. Another upside of it was that she hadn't let go of him since then. She'd slipped her arm into his and leaned against him as if she was meant to be there. Amazing what throwing yourself off a building can do for a friendship. Never mind the libido. 'They've closed the jump shop for today, sweetie. Stop pouting. Maybe we can go another day. If you're good.'

'I can be.'

'I know.' He saw the flicker of need there, heard

it in her voice. But he'd promised himself he'd take it slowly with her. She'd had a point earlier—they needed to learn how to communicate. Good sex could only get better when two people knew each other well, right? After that, he didn't know. Distance hadn't worked for him. Maybe getting to know her, discovering all the faults that he could find in her, maybe that would dampen down this incessant craving to be with her.

Yeah, she must have faults. Trouble was, he hadn't found any yet.

He walked her down past the city-centre shops, along the waterfront, stopping to point out the old harbour buildings nestled between new glass-fronted architecture. Tourists spilled from the cruise ship, smiling and laughing, some dancing to the buskers beating out an old popular song. There was a carnival atmosphere.

He squeezed her to him as they strolled, ignoring the guilt that he should be doing paperwork or preparing for a lecture he was giving to the undergrads tomorrow morning. And the fact he really didn't know what he was offering her here. 'There are a few cool bars over there where we can grab something to eat. This area's changed heaps over the years. It used to be just a working dock.'

'You know a lot about the place. Is this where you grew up?'

Although he usually felt uncomfortable talking about his past, he let it go. He could hardly encourage her to embrace new things without trying a few himself. Besides, she had this way of asking in such a way that he couldn't help wanting to give her answers. 'I'm a Jaffa, yeah—Just Another Fella From Auckland. I went to Marquis School in the city.'

'Marquis, eh? Very posh. You rich, then?'

He laughed at her forthrightness. 'Not really. Just circumstances. Then I had a few years at Otago University. A couple in Aussie, learning the trade. Then back here.' He chose not to dwell on the early part of his life.

'Did you both go to Otago?'

'Both?'

'You and Mitch. Duh.'

She often spoke about him and his twin as if they were joined at the hip. How to explain that from the age of six he'd been brought up as an only child? Any time he told anyone the truth it was greeted with too much pity. He didn't need that. 'Yes. We did the same course. It's the best med school in the country.'

'Must have been hard on everyone else there, all that Maitland alpha ego and rivalry. A real force to be reckoned with. Now look at you, both top docs in your field, at such a young age.'

'Yeah, right.' He didn't mean to put an awkward silence in there. But somehow it had happened. His tone had been too sharp, too quick.

He didn't know what to say next and he definitely didn't want to delve too deeply into the dark side and deflate her high, so he gripped her hand and steered her into an Asian fusion restaurant overlooking the millionaires' yachts in the Viaduct harbour.

The lights from the buildings reflected in the dark water, giving the place an eerie glow. Bittersweet memories dallied with his heartstrings. This was the last place he'd seen his parents, so it was kind of spooky and special in equal measure. 'Wine? Mojito?'

'For a non-date, you're trying pretty hard to woo me.' She cast him a sarcastic smile. 'Lemonade, please.'

He ignored the jibe. Some called it wooing, he called it trying to be friendly. 'You sure you don't want a mojito?'

'No. I've got a bit of residual stomach griping

from that vomiting bug.' Swiping her hand across her abdomen, she smiled. 'No biggie.'

'Yeah, it hit everyone hard. Took some of my interns weeks to get over it, or so they said. I thought they were just pulling my string.' Underneath those rosy cheeks he saw shadows. 'You okay, though?'

'Fine.' And now she looked embarrassed to be talking about herself like that.

He took her to a table, ordered the drinks and let the subject drop. 'So what about you, Gabby? You trained in Wellington?'

'Yes. It was a bit of a hike, travelling in every day, but I didn't want to leave Mum and Nonna to do all the work at home.'

'And yet here you are.'

'I know. The black sheep.' She blushed. He got the feeling she was picking her words carefully. This was obviously difficult territory for her. 'I still feel bad, but I just had to leave. I couldn't bear it anymore.'

'Why?'

'Oh…' Again she seemed cagey and unsure but also like it was a relief to let it out. 'My mum and I haven't got on for years, but I stayed for Nonna. Because of Nonna. When she died a few months ago I decided it was time to start fresh somewhere else. So I chose here.' Her words tumbled out in a stream and he was grateful she'd chosen him to confide in. More than grateful, especially when he knew he'd struggle to do the same with her—with anyone.

When he looked deeper into her eyes he saw a flicker of trust there—tiny and wavering, but there. And for a moment he didn't know if he could bear that responsibility when he couldn't give it back. Something in his chest constricted but he directed his focus on her. This was about Gabby. Not him. 'Was your mum happy about that?'

'My mum is generally not happy about anything I do.' She laughed, but it wasn't forced, more like she accepted her lot. 'She's not a coper, and relied on me and Nonna for way too much. But I decided she needed to learn how to stand on her own two feet. Actually, I decided to be the adult, so I enlisted some cheap labour to help her out and then I came here. So let's just say I left under a cloud. But it's nothing new. I had a lot of those growing up.'

'Why?'

'Lots of reasons—I was a surprise, not a happy

one. Then I was the great hope. Mum was a single parent. We had little cash. I was…' she raised her eyebrows '…*destined for great things*. Mum and Nonna pegged me to be a doctor and buy them out of their financial mess. It's safe to say I let them down.'

'But being a nurse isn't a let-down.' Although the pain behind her eyes told him there was something she wasn't telling him. Something deep that still hurt now. Had she failed her exams? Had she not been cut out for it? Had she plain not wanted to be a doctor? 'Believe me, I know it's hard to carry the hopes of those around with you. Never quite meeting expectations, always feeling that you'd failed.' He knew all about not being good enough. No wonder they shared a connection.

'Not being a doctor is more than a let-down in their eyes. My having an independent mind and spirit never sat easily with them. I was raised to do what I was told and be a good girl. Or else…' She toyed with her silver necklace, ran her fingers over the diamond locket. 'Okay, spotlight back on Max.'

'Ugh.' He took a drink. 'You are far more interesting. Do we have to?'

'Yes. Parents?'

'Obviously. It's difficult to be alive without them.'

'Thank you for that, Mr Maitland. I can see why you became a doctor. I bet you aced biology.' The death stare returned, albeit laced with a laugh. 'Your parents are where?'

Before he could sugar-coat it the word tripped off his tongue. Flat. Cold. 'Dead.'

'Oh.' Fiddling with the napkin, she dipped her head, bit along the bottom of her lip. 'Gosh. I'm sorry.'

'Don't be. It was a very long time ago.' He'd gotten over it. Gotten over the fact they'd waved goodbye and that had been the last he'd seen of them. That a few days later he'd said goodbye to his brother, too. His whole damned world had fallen apart and he'd been unable to understand any of it. 'It was a yachting accident. They were planning to sail from here to Fiji but got caught up in a storm and didn't survive.'

'How old were you?'

'Six.'

She looked like she was about to throw up. Tears threatened as she leaned forward and stroked his hair. 'That's terrible. You poor things. I can't imagine—'

'You ready to order?' Worse than the thick weight pressing on his chest was seeing the pity in her eyes. Hurt was bad enough. 'I heard the wagyu is delicious.'

'Whatever you think.' Her hand dropped as she stared at the menu. Obviously his clumsy shift in conversation topic had upset her.

Damn, he'd done it again. Driven a wedge through a perfectly innocent conversation. They were supposed to be getting to know each other, but he didn't know how to bare his soul. He'd held it all in for so long it was part of him. And he didn't feel ready to give her that part just yet.

With impeccable timing his phone hit top decibels.

Mitchell. The name flashed on the display and he knew Gabby saw it too. Mitchell never rang. Ever. So this was important.

But Gabby stared up at him with those huge wide eyes that showed a flash of irritation. Max knew he was walking a tightrope here, and he wanted to get it right. 'I'll leave it.'

'No. Take it. It might be important.'

'No way. I'm not falling for that one.' Smiling, he pushed the phone into the middle of the table. 'I know this test—it's double-woman-speak for "answer that and I spear you with this steak knife".'

She pushed the phone back, her eyes warmer now. 'Seriously, take it. You've more than learnt your lesson. But next time, any trouble and you're off that Sky Tower without the harness, right?'

Truthfully, Gabby didn't mind at all. Not if it was Mitchell ringing. The intense adrenalin of the jump, then the opposite slump of devastation at hearing Max's story had jumbled her up, and she was glad for a few moments' respite.

The more she learnt about him, the more he seemed to entrance her. Fabulous yet arrogant surgeon he may be, but he came from such tragedy. That could be the reason for his dedication and need to succeed. Motivation came from so many different sources—maybe he was looking for validation through his work. Through sex—he certainly made a success of that. But that didn't account for all the problems between him and his brother.

Oh, stop the amateur psychology and stop trying to read into things. What she did know was that the poor twins must have gone through hell. Her dad had never been in her life so she'd never missed him, but to lose both parents at the same time was devastating. And they'd been so young.

Who'd looked after them from the age of six? How had two little boys coped with the deaths of their parents? And had any of that had anything to do with their rift?

Staring out over the water, she pretended she was fascinated by the view, tapped her foot to the jazzy music in the background. All the time straining to hear what Max could possibly be saying to his brother.

His voice had become calm after an initial hardness. 'Not tonight. No. Another time. Soon, though.' He paused, seemed to look for words. 'Thanks, anyway.'

Not wanting to pry, she smiled—okay, she did want to pry, itched to pry, really truly desperately ached to pry, she had so many questions she didn't know where to start, so couldn't—and waited for Max to speak. When he just stared at the phone in some kind of daze, she coughed.

He blinked and gave her a funny half-hearted smile back. Suddenly he seemed so boyish her heart snagged. For all his sophisticated suaveness the guy had issues that ran deep, and he was obviously still working through them. 'That was weird. Mitchell has a night off tonight and wondered if I wanted to go round for a drink.'

'Oh? You should go, then.'

'Here we go again with the test. No.' He picked up the menu and scanned it. 'I'm not having you run out on me again.'

'Seriously, this is good news, isn't it? You should go before you both lose your nerve or find something else to argue about. Like who has the most bubbles in your damn lemonade.'

'But I'm here with you. You're *important*.'

'I can wait.' Laughing, she rubbed her shoulder. Since the jump she'd had a niggling pain there—probably pulled a muscle or something. In fact, generally she felt pretty wiped out with the adrenalin high leaching out of her system. She just wanted to crash. 'Seriously, I'm not really hungry. You go and see Mitchell and I'll head off to bed.'

She stood to go. The room swam around and she grabbed the table edge. 'Whoa.'

'You okay?'

'Low blood pressure, I guess.' The nausea swirled. When she could focus again she let go. It was definitely a good idea to go home, although it would be a shame to let the evening come to an end. But there would be more of him tomorrow.

More tiny steps forward. 'I'm fine. But I really think I need an early night.'

'Alone?'

'Yes. Alone, Max.' She tutted, then looped her arm into his as they walked to the main road. He was such a muddle of contradictions. One minute he was intense and sad. The next he was cracking jokes about sex. He'd moved on swiftly from his dark mood. If only he'd give her the whole story. Then she'd truly feel like she understood him. But there was a way to go before that happened. 'This has been the best night, but we're still learning.'

'We could learn a lot faster…naked.'

Yes, please. She batted his arm, shoving away thoughts of how good he looked wearing absolutely nothing. Nonna had always taught her that you had to wait for your rewards because they tasted all the more sweet. Gabby hoped like hell Nonna was right. 'So, how did we do? You think you might want to do this again another night?'

'Well, we have the team kayaking trip tomorrow evening.' His eyebrows rose cheekily. 'Some watersport is always interesting to add to the sexy mix.'

'Do you really think about sex every five minutes?'

'Sex with you? Every three.'

'Honestly! You're incorrigible.' But she smiled. The fact he still wanted her and cared enough to let her know made her feel hot inside. She'd never had that—had thought she'd had it once with Isaac but that had been a fallacy.

Truth was, she didn't really want to go home alone. She didn't want him to go off and see his brother. She wanted to lie in his arms and go to sleep. But she knew if they spent another night together she would be committing herself to him. And that would mean opening her heart, her old wounds, her memories. And she wasn't ready for that. She didn't know if she ever could be.

'Let me take you home first.' His arms circled her waist and he pecked a nonchalant kiss on the tip of her nose. 'I'm worried about you. You don't look well.'

'I'm fine. Please, get to your brother's before it's too late.'

A taxi pulled up and he opened the door for her, paid the fare in advance and blew her a kiss. But as he disappeared into the darkness, her heart constricted.

It was already too late. Somewhere along the

line she'd committed her heart to him and she couldn't do a darned thing about it.

She fiddled with her necklace, clenched the diamond in her fist. But then what? If she was going to let him like her, and have a decent chance at a relationship, she'd have to be honest, tell him what she'd done all those years ago.

And she couldn't do that. She just couldn't.

CHAPTER NINE

BAD IDEA.

Max squeezed the beer can in his hand while his brother left the room to tend to Jamie. Getting together with Mitch was always difficult. Growing up, they hadn't played board games, they'd played barbed games. Who could hurt who the most. Who could be the bolder, bigger, braver. Who was the best.

Distance had put paid to any kind of relationship. Hundreds of kilometres and lack of desire on their uncles' behalf to allow them time together had forced them apart. Until that distance had become insurmountable, geographically and emotionally.

On the few occasions they'd spent time together Max had been eaten away with envy at the cosy family set-up Mitchell had compared to his own stark, harsh one—and how little his brother had needed him. He'd believed Mitchell had had no space in his life for his twin. And that hurt had dissolved into anger. At Mitch. At the world.

He knew Mitch had been jealous of him too— jealous of the money, luxuries Mitchell's family couldn't afford. Gradually that mutual jealousy, fuelled by their uncles' own dislike of each other, had poisoned them against each other.

So he should have listened to his gut and stayed with Gabby. But, for Jamie's sake, he had to try. And he knew if Gabby got wind of any kind of worsening of relations between him and his twin there'd be hell to pay.

Hell, since when had he answered to a woman?

Since he'd fallen, literally, for a stubborn, newly signed-up member of the adrenalin-junkie club.

The door swung open and Mitch reappeared. Like looking into a mirror, Max could read his brother's moods, his emotions. Today they connected somewhere round about clueless. Mitch sat down in a big leather chair that had seen better decades, his hands curled round a can. 'Max, I think it's time we sorted a few things out.'

'Jodi put you up to this?'

'Yes. And no.' Mitch at least looked like he was trying to find the right words. 'You saved our boy's life and I can't thank you enough for that. I really can't. I owe you. We all do.'

'It's my job,' Max countered. But they both knew it was more than that.

'Thing is, now Jodi has this fantasy that we'll all live happily ever after.'

'Is there such a thing?'

'I hope so. For my son's sake.' The guy looked exhausted. He'd had a hell of a few months, getting acquainted with a child he hadn't known existed and reconnecting with a woman he'd separated from some years ago. In reality both brothers had had a hell of a time—their whole lives. They were the only ones who understood what the other was going through, and yet were unable to make things right.

Mitchell's family had always been plagued by money worries. Max had hoped he could help ease the way a little. He took a deep breath, unsure how Mitchell would take this. 'I wanted to tell you, I've set up a trust fund for Jamie.'

'You've done what?' It was hard to read his reaction. 'I don't need your money.'

'Hear me out. I wanted to give him something and I didn't know what. I thought it might help.'

Mitch's fist closed around his can and the metal

twisted and bulged. 'Because you don't think I can provide?'

'No. I just thought—'

'That you could do better?' Mitchell's eyes blackened. Ease the way? Laughable. Seemed he'd erected a roadblock. 'That'd be right. You haven't got a son, so you thought you'd buy mine?'

But then Mitchell looked as shocked as Max felt. What to say now? There was nothing to reply to that.

A wavering silence descended. Max studied his shoes. Mitch stared at the wall.

Eventually Mitch leaned forward and shook his head. 'I shouldn't have said that. I was out of order.'

It was Mitch-speak for *I'm sorry*. Max took it gladly. 'Look, I know things weren't great for you financially growing up, that you're still sorting out things for your...for Uncle Harry.'

Mitch laughed. 'Yeah, I got the bum run there. Should have been picked by Fred.'

'No, we should never have been in that situation at all. Two uncles given a choice—*a choice*—as to which boy they'd have. Like picking out a new car or a house. *Dip dip dip. My blue ship.*'

So they'd been boisterous and grief-stricken and

a handful. So they'd fought and screamed and missed their mum and dad. So they'd run away, lashed out and cried. But no one should ever have split twins up so soon after their parents' death.

What the hell had been going on in the grown-ups' heads he had no idea—but it had been obvious to Max then, as a child, that their decisions were so wrong. So horribly wrong. And in true Maitland style the uncles had been fighting their own battles. Who was better than who? Who was most successful? Who had the better son? One-upmanship ran deep in the genes. They'd all been living with the consequences ever since.

Max spoke up, 'Harry tried hard, though, didn't he? I was always envious of you—you seemed to have a connection with them and their kids. All I had was a fancy education from Fred's Midas touch.'

'Lucky you.' Mitch sat back in his chair. 'You did well out of his cash.'

'Lucky?' Max remembered the frequent emotional blackmail and taunts. *We never asked for you. We didn't want kids.* How Max would never ever be good enough in Fred's eyes. Compared to Mitchell's poor but loving upbringing it certainly had never felt like he'd won the jackpot. Rich, yes. But desperately alone.

'No, Mitch, there's a lot more to life than money. I didn't feel lucky at all. All our lives you've compared what you had to what I had. You have no idea what it was like.'

'To struggle? To have to work hard? To try to be as good as your brother? Get real, Max. You had a charmed life.'

Although this was getting out of control, it was getting real too. Finally opening up about what they'd both endured. Was it his imagination or did his back still sting from his uncle's belt wound twenty-odd years ago? Hiding the reality from everyone was preferable to reliving it. 'It wasn't easy for me. Stuff happened.'

'What kind of stuff?'

'You don't want to know.' But Max didn't want to sound like a victim either. 'Forget it. Let's move on.'

Because that's what happened in their lives. People moved on, leaving emptiness, chaos and hurt. Which was why Max never invested in his emotions. He never again wanted to feel the way he had when he'd lost his parents and then his brother. His enduring memory was of being dragged away, his brother's screams stinging in his ears.

From somewhere in the small townhouse Jamie cried out, the noise echoing off the walls.

Following his brother out to the hall, Max decided it was time to leave. He'd tried. They'd both tried. Who knew if it was enough?

Just before he left, Max paused, his hand on the doorhandle. 'Just one thing, Mitch. Do you remember making a den out of sheets and the clothes airer?'

Mitchell shook his head and frowned. 'No. Why?'

'In the lounge. In our old house?'

'No.'

'Really? A den that we slept in one night. And we had a secret language that used to drive Mum mad, you must remember that?'

'Nah.' Mitch's shoulders lifted then dropped as he turned to mount the stairs. 'It was too long ago. I've got a new life now, I'm trying to make a go of it. Like you, I'm trying to forget all that stuff.'

Max let himself out, a heavy ache thickening across his chest. Maybe it was pointless to even try to reach out to his twin, to try to create a family. Not when they didn't even have the same memories.

* * *

When the phone rang Gabby was sitting on the floor of her closet, sorting through her memory boxes again. Even though he wasn't in the room she instinctively closed the closet door to hide them from view. 'Max?'

'Hey.' Although it was wonderful to hear his voice, it filled her with concern. He sounded flat. Tired. In the restaurant he'd been so closed down she hadn't known how to handle it. All she could do was wait until he was ready to talk. 'Thought I'd ring and see how you are.'

'I'm okay,' she lied, infusing brightness into her voice to counteract his. That damned SkyJump had snagged something in her stomach as well as her shoulder. An ache she couldn't shake with regular painkillers, which only zapped her strength and humour. Maybe she wasn't cut out to be an extreme adventurist just yet, or it needed a level of fitness more than that of a flea. 'How did it go with Maitland Two?'

'In his eyes he's Maitland One—so don't be surprised if that nickname isn't a hit.' His laugh was hollow and it made her heart hitch. She imagined him in that huge empty apartment with nothing for company but the plants and his worsening mood. 'To be honest, it went exactly as I expected.'

Not good, then. 'You need a distraction. Why don't you step outside and busy yourself with watering the babies?'

'Thanks. But I don't think that will help.' His voice thawed a little.

'So, what would?'

'You.' So inevitable. So obvious. So honest. His breathing stilled as he waited for her answer.

She glanced at the clock, torn between looking after herself and giving him what he needed. Maybe he needed to talk. Maybe they'd end up back at nothing—where neither felt able to give any more. But she'd spent a lifetime doing things for other people, rightly or wrongly—now she felt a tug of responsibility for him too.

It wasn't a bad thing, though, far from it. She liked it. She wanted to wipe that sadness from his voice, knew they'd have a fun time. That if anyone could make him feel better tonight, it was her. There was no point denying it: she'd lost a piece of her heart to him. And maybe, just maybe, he'd done the same with her.

But if she went over now, there'd be no going back. The commitment would be there, blatant in her actions. He'd know it. And so would she. 'I'd love to, Max. But I have an early shift tomorrow then the kayak trip straight after. I need to get some good sleep. I'm bushed.'

There was another long pause while he weighed up her answer. He breathed out a sigh, 'Okay, sure. I understand. No worries. See you tomorrow, then.' Then he hung up.

Just like that. Max Maitland had hung up with no sexual innuendo. No cheeky repartee.

The man had hung up without a fight.

Damn.

Ten minutes later she leaned against his apartment doorbell, letting it ring until he answered it. 'Surprised?'

He didn't speak. He was wearing the faded T-shirt from before and tight washed-out jeans. He looked like something from an advert, surly and sullen. But relieved.

His blue, blue eyes stared at her with a kind of need and tenderness that she'd never experienced before. Like she'd saved his world. Like there was nothing else he wanted more in his life.

Pressing her into his arms, his lips hit hers with a force that snatched her breath away. He hauled her against the door as his mouth traced rough, greedy kisses over her cheeks, her neck, her throat. His passion ignited a desire in her that overrode her intentions, overrode her sensibilities. All the holding back and the frustrations and the fear of letting herself go entirely with him were shot. He needed her and she needed him right back.

'I want you. My God, Gabby, I want you so much.' His hands clawed at her blouse, ripped it from her, dragged her skirt to the floor. 'I want to be inside you. Now.'

'Yes. Yes.' She couldn't, wouldn't deny him this. She reached for his T-shirt, threw it to the floor. Tugged at his belt, her fingers brushing against his hardness. She needed him now as much as he needed her. Once she'd freed his erection from the constraints of his jeans she took him in her hand, felt the heat, the strength of him.

'God. Don't…' He groaned into her ear. 'Wait. Please.'

His fingers parted her legs, slipped into her, sending jolts of pleasure spiralling through her body. His mouth met hers again and he kissed her long and hard, stoking the want. If she didn't have him, if she didn't…she'd die. Pure and simple.

A huge pressure built inside her and all she could see, feel, hear was him. Max. His smell. His touch. And her whole body craved him.

'Now. I want you now.' Her voice was cracked and desperate, her words coming between each tight thrust of his fingers.

All too soon he withdrew them, cupped her bottom with both hands and picked her up. She wrapped her legs around his thighs and positioned herself over him. Then he was sliding into her. Pounding her against the wall, hard and fast.

He gazed at her as he entered her, a different Max now from any she'd ever seen before—emboldened and savage. Glorious and powerful. And he wanted *her*. Wanted to bury himself inside *her*. Wanted to lose himself and his crazy mixed-up feelings in *her*.

She squeezed tightly around him, gripped his back. Felt ripped apart with emotion—the intensity of his need meshing with her own. The ache in her stomach waned, then intensified with every stroke.

Those cool Maitland eyes bored into her, making a million promises. That connection she never believed she'd have. That fusion of souls.

Harder. Faster. He pounded.

Just when she thought she couldn't handle any more he tensed then moaned into her hair. Long and loud. She bucked against him, reaching the same high. Higher. Higher. Until the world splintered and burst into tiny stars.

He held her against the wall, rocking with her, slowly, slowly, his forehead against hers as their erratic breathing steadied. His kisses were more gentle now, infused with tenderness.

A huge knot of emotion lodged in her chest. She wanted him. Wanted Max Maitland more than anything else in the world.

She wanted him fiercely. Desperately. She wanted him to hold her heart and treasure it, not trash it like Isaac and Nonna and her mother had done. And she would hold and treasure his, if he offered it to her. If he could make that step. If she could.

After a few minutes she was able to speak. 'That was the most amazing thing.'

'Yeah. And so are you.' He withdrew and wrapped her in his arms. 'Come to bed. And this time you are not allowed to leave without me. No sneaking off. Promise?'

'Promise. I'll stay as long as you want.'
Forever?

He carried her through to the bedroom as if she were as light as candyfloss and fitted himself around her, pulling cool sheets over their spent bodies. She watched as his eyelids fluttered closed.

'Don't go to sleep just yet, Max,' she whispered into the darkness. 'Tell me about it.'

'What?' His eyes remained closed but he snuggled in closer and rested his chin on her head.

'Mitchell.'

'Oh, you know. Same old, same old.'

She sighed. Was he hedging? Or did he truly not understand what she meant? The way she saw it, the only thing holding Max back from committing to anything was Mitch. And their tragic past. And she understood his reluctance to share his story. After all, history held her back, too. But she needed that connection with him. 'I mean from the beginning. Tell me about the geography. What happened after your parents…went?'

Against her chest his heartbeat sped up. 'It's too long and too late.'

'I won't go to sleep until you talk. And you know I have that kind of willpower.' She nudged him gently and wiggled round to face him. 'You want to try me?'

'No, I know what you're capable of, scary nurse lady.' He inhaled deeply, the hollows and slants of his face darker and more defined in the moon-lit room. He was clearly filtering the information before he spoke.

He swallowed slowly, then began. 'Okay, so after our parents died we were put in care. Just for a short while. We were distraught and a handful. And I mean a handful.' He laughed sadly. 'But we just didn't understand what had happened. They weren't coming back, the people kept telling us. What did that mean?'

She imagined the two boys, not much older than Jamie, vulnerable and scared, living in a stranger's house. Tears pricked the backs of her eyes. 'It must have been terrifying.'

'Not as bad as then finding out we were going to live in separate homes.'

'What? Why?'

His hand stroked her thigh, back and forth. Back and forth. The rhythm seemed to steady him. 'My father had two brothers. Seems they were put in a difficult situation by the authorities—someone had to take us. And pretty damned soon before we got too difficult and they couldn't place us anywhere.

'Our uncles had always argued, played the Maitland competitive games. Neither of them really wanted us and they couldn't agree who'd take us both. So, as they couldn't reach a happy compromise to keep us together, they agreed to take one each.'

'That's ridiculous.'

'It is what it is.'

'So you were grieving and then separated. Twins? It's ludicrous.'

'It was almost thirty years ago; things are different now. Back then it was about keeping the adults happy. No one thought about how we'd cope.' He shuddered. It was obviously traumatic for him to talk about this—but it explained so much about him. How he kept parts of himself hidden from public view and wouldn't even allow a private glimpse. Why he chose to flit from woman to woman instead of putting down roots. He didn't know how. Probably too damned scared that every single person he formed an attachment to would leave him.

'The worst thing I remember was being led away by Fred. I could hear Mitch calling for me.

I wanted to run to him, to tell him that whatever happened I'd find him and we'd be together again. But I was too scared, they were adults and they were in charge. Fred wasn't the type of man you messed with. And I was the older brother, I was supposed to look after Mitch. But I couldn't. I couldn't stop what they were doing. And I couldn't bear to see the look on his face as I lost him, too.'

Her heart was breaking. She gripped his hand and encouraged him to speak again, hoping that some good would come out of letting out all that pent-up hurt. 'You must have seen him again, though? Surely? They wouldn't keep you separated for long? That would be criminal.'

'Over the years Mitch and I got to see each other less and less. One year Harry and Fred had an almighty blow-up and access was pretty much stopped altogether. When we did ever meet up it was like being with a stranger, a distant cousin. His life was so different. So full, with brothers and sisters. He didn't need me. And I was completely alone. It wasn't until university, when we met up again, that it totally came to a head. Over Jodi.'

Hence the reality in which they lived now. It all slotted into place. 'What about your aunties?'

'My Aunty Beryl—*Mum*—they adopted me so they made me call her that—was nice enough.'

At the word 'adopted' Gabby froze.

She grappled to find words to fill his pause, but couldn't find anything to say. Her throat had closed. She nodded against his chin, encouraged him to go on.

'She was meek and subservient to Fred and did whatever he told her to. And he was a bully—I grew to hate him. Nothing was good enough. He once told me he wished he'd never agreed to take me on. Kids were too much trouble.' He huffed out a breath, his body shaking with anger. 'I was supposed to call them Mum and Dad—they were supposed to be my parents. Can you imagine? Can anyone replace your real parents? The ones who love you unconditionally?'

God, she hoped so. She really, truly did. His story had so many echoes of her own it broke her heart.

For the last ten years she'd desperately hoped that parental love could come naturally to those who wanted it enough. But what if it didn't? What if they changed their minds? What if they decided their child wasn't what they'd dreamt it could be? What if they made life intolerable?

The pain she'd carried around for so long almost overwhelmed her. This was Max's story, not hers, but she grieved for him with every bit of her heart. He'd lost. She'd lost, too. But while he'd had all choice whipped away, she'd made the choice on her own. And with good cause.

He hauled her close, kissed the top of her head, his heat and strength cocooning her.

She was utterly torn between holding him close and fighting free from his grip. To stay in his heat, and get away from him so she could stop more hurt. She wanted to be alone with her memories and her thoughts. She wanted to scream. To run. To stay. To weep.

Her throat closed, her belly hurt. God, how her belly hurt—a tight knot of emotion that squeezed and twisted.

His voice was hard now. 'My parents sailed off on some second honeymoon trip. They were supposed to be gone a few months, but they never came back. How could they do that? How could they happily leave us with a nanny for so long? How could they go off and die and give us up to strangers?' He nuzzled closer, took three deep breaths as he calmed down. It seemed like an age before he moved or spoke.

She wondered if he'd fallen asleep, but no way could anyone rest with such rage surging through him.

Eventually, he whispered, 'I'm sorry—you didn't need to hear all this stuff. You must think I'm crazy. But you could say I got pretty messed up back then. Every child has a right to be loved, right? To be brought up by parents who love them more than anything in the world? Who won't harm them? Who treasure them? There is no end of hurt, knowing you aren't wanted.'

That was when she knew she had to leave.

She had to walk away and not look back.

Judging by his intense emotions and his cruel experience, Max would never understand how she'd been able to do what she had. How she'd believed the choices she'd made had been for the best.

She needed to put space between herself and Max. Had to get out of his life once and for all, and never, ever let him know her story.

CHAPTER TEN

'Hey, would you look at that? I just realised we left my apartment together. At the same time,' Max whispered, when he approached Gabby at the nurses' station. All day he'd thought of nothing but having a rerun of last night. As he remembered her legs wrapped round his waist, his grin spread inwards and through him like a light.

Having opened his heart to her, he felt pretty damned good—like they'd made headway into something important. But he felt disoriented, too, on shaky ground. Like any minute now he'd get the need to run. Far away.

Trouble was, she seemed a bit subdued. Had been very quiet over breakfast. Uttered hardly a word as he'd dropped her off on the way to his ward round. Had barely managed a kiss. She was probably tired, so he needed to pep her up. 'Must be a sign.'

'Of what?' She looked up at him as she wrote

patient details on a large whiteboard. Dark circles edged her eyes.

'Good things. I don't know. You didn't sneak out. That has to be good, right?' Watching her buckle slightly as she reached up, he leapt forward. 'Hey, are you okay?'

'Watch it, Prince Charming.' She nodded and backed out of his arms. 'It's busy and I don't want anyone to see us like this. I'm fine, it's just women's stuff, you know.'

Ah. He knew not to say a word. Just nodded. Took a step or two out of range. He hadn't known her long enough or well enough to know how she coped with periods, whether she got PMS, whether she growled like a bad-tempered lioness once a month. Heck, he didn't know her favourite colour, what she ate for breakfast. Sweet or savoury. Coffee or tea.

But he looked forward to learning more about her. What he did know was that he couldn't keep away from her. That she was the first woman ever to hold his attention for more than a few days. Weeks.

And he sure as hell needed to rein his enthusiasm in. Tiny steps, like she said. 'Okay, got you. Enough said. I've got stuff to do, anyway. I'll pick you up in thirty minutes or so for the kayak trip. There's a bunch of us going down to the bay in my car.'

'I don't think I'm up to it. I'm still feeling grotty.'

Having been in hibernation way too long, his possessive instinct pushed to centre stage, as it always did whenever Nurse Radley came onto his radar. 'Do you think you should get it checked out?'

'Being over-protective?' She threw him a small smile. 'I'm twenty-five. I've been dealing with this stuff a long time. I get heavy periods, that's why I'm on the Pill—not so I can pick up strange men in bars and have random sex. Right? And now you know way too much about me. I just need a cup of tea, my bed and a hottie.'

'At your service.' He gave her a low bow, raised his head in time to see the frown. 'Okay, I get it, not that kind of hottie.'

'You are so up yourself. Now go away and let me work. And I'll definitely give the kayaking a miss. Can you tell Rach?'

'Tell me about what?' Rachel wandered over, the expression on her face telling him that their attempts at keeping their liaisons secret were failing. She winked. 'We have news?'

'Gabby's not feeling great so she's going to cry off the trip this arvo.'

Rachel's face fell. It was clearly not the kind of news she was anticipating. 'Not you, too? We're getting very short on numbers. If we're not careful we'll have to cancel altogether.' Then she seemed to realise how callous that must have sounded. 'Gosh. Sorry. I mean, if you're not up to it then we can postpone until next month or something.'

He watched a flurry of emotions flutter over Gabby's face. She looked first at Rachel then at Max, then back to Rachel. Absently rubbing her hand across her stomach, she shrugged. 'Oh, okay, okay. I don't want to let you all down. I'll come. But be gentle with me, and bags I get that two-man canoe.'

Standing at the water's edge at Okahu Bay, Gabby looked over at the majestic humped-top island. Rangitoto, an extinct volcano now covered in bush, appeared almost close enough to touch. But she knew it would take more than an hour to get over there by kayak. That was on a good day.

Today was not a good day. She felt strangely light-headed at the thought of expending energy on anything. Her legs didn't feel strong enough to hold her up, never mind keep her stable on a long paddle across an ocean, and the dragging sensation in her belly had worsened.

Maybe a workout would help soothe the pain, or at least take her mind off it.

As long as she kept a reasonable distance from Max. Confused didn't describe how she felt— more like she'd lost something precious and knew she'd never be able to find it again. Her heart ached for him, but her head knew it was better if she kept him at arm's length.

Her attempts at avoiding him were in vain, as usual. Maybe it was time to move on, get a new job somewhere else, a different unit, hospital. A different country. At least then she wouldn't have to face him every day knowing that things could have been so good.

Dragging on the lifejacket, she had a weird feeling of dropping. The island blurred, then came back into focus. Then blurred again. Her head pounded and the pain in her stomach stabbed and dragged.

'Looks like it's you and me in this one.' Max hauled a double kayak towards the water. 'Hop in.'

'I was thinking I'd go with Rach or something—

you know, sisters doing it for themselves and all that.' She raised a weak fist.

'I think your *sister* has other things on her mind.' He nodded over to where Rachel was climbing into a kayak with Rob from the night shift. She looked very cosy and not the least sisterly. Giggling even. *Traitor.* Max grinned and handed Gabby a paddle. 'We'd better be quick or we'll be the last to set off.'

'And that would be bad, why?'

'Because we'd lose.'

'Is everything a competition to you?'

'You say it like it's a bad thing.' Dropping the kayak into the shallows he turned, strode over to her and zipped up her lifejacket. Made sure it was fastened and she would be safe. Damn him. Did he have to be so considerate? Could he not be difficult? Did she have to be turned on by everything he did?

His fingers ran along the lifejacket, skimming the sides of her breasts. Instinctively they pebbled, anticipating his touch.

She edged out of reach. 'Don't…'

'What's all this about? Are you okay?'

'Yes. But I'm uncomfortable with people seeing us like this. And this kind of makes it obvious.' And too darned hard for her to cope with. Next thing she knew she'd be kissing him in full view of everyone.

'Sure, because they all look totally bound up in our lives, don't they? We could be naked and they wouldn't notice.'

'I would.' *Hell, yes.* For all the wrong reasons. She loved to see his long sun-kissed lithe legs, his perfect bum, his broad chest. And now she was torturing herself with such delicious images.

She glanced over at the team. They were jabbering about the trip, pushing off into the sparkling water. Planning their picnic and volcano walk. He was right. No one even seemed to notice that she and Max were in the same hemisphere, let alone same kayak.

'Okay.' Time to pull on the big girl's pants again. She would do this one trip. To keep everyone happy and bolster the team. Then she would be honest and open with him. Explain how things could not work—especially in light of what he'd told her of his past and his fervent beliefs. Then they would both be able to move on.

The trip across the harbour was smooth, the water calm, and the dappled late-afternoon sunlight provided a gentle warmth that was nurturing rather than overwhelming.

Unlike Maitland One. 'How easy is it to have sex in one of these things, do you think?'

She almost dropped the paddle. 'Impossible. Especially with all the rocking. Don't go there, Max.'

'That would make it more fun, don't you think? Living on the brink.' His voice deepened to that irresistible groan that stoked her inside. 'You want to try?'

Yes, please. 'Max, I'm wedged into a two-foot-wide hole and I'm soaking wet. There's about fifty metres of water between me and the ground. And...' She gestured to the flotilla of sailing boats with their white sails fluttering in the wind. 'There are more sailing boats and kayaks around than America's Cup week. I do not have sex with an audience.'

'So I take it from that you're possibly not keen? Wavering maybe?' His laughter fanned the flames his voice ignited. Damn him. One day she'd look at him and find nothing attractive about him at all. She would. She prayed that day would come soon. Tomorrow? And in that tight navy T-shirt and bright blue boardies, did he have to define sexy, too? The man would look sexy in a paper bag.

He kept right on laughing. And stoking. 'Look, I want to talk to you about something. I do need your help.'

'Oh, yes?' She tried for nonchalant, wasn't sure she could ever be nonchalant around him.

But any call for help and she was there.

'I've been nominated for an award at the hospital annual ball and I need a plus-one. How about you come with me?' he yelled now, as he pulled back effortlessly on the paddles, propelling them fast and furious into the path of another kayaker. He really did want to win. In everything. Thing was, she had trouble denying him, too. But she had to.

'No, thanks.' She offered him a smile. Firm and fair. And as honest as she could be right now. 'I can't. I've nothing to wear.'

'You look fine like that.'

Whacking the paddle onto the surface of the ocean, she sent an arc of water behind her. Hopefully hitting her target. 'In cut-off denim shorts and an old T-shirt? Yeah, right. Perfect evening wear.'

'You'd look amazing in anything. Hell, you look amazing in nothing.'

He was making this very hard for her. How was

she supposed to tell him it was finished when he said things like that? When he made her feel the things she did? Sexy. Desirable.

Want flickered around her nerve endings, tripped up her spine, spread to her breasts, her groin. She tried to ignore it, even though it was getting way past troublesome. 'New charge nurse attends ball in birthday suit—that would get tongues wagging.' She tutted. 'I'm sorry, no. But you could advertise in the hospital classifieds. *Mr Sexy needs a date.* I'm sure you'd get plenty of offers.'

'I don't want plenty. I want you.' Even though he was behind her she could feel the swell of his chest. 'Mr Sexy, eh? Come on, say yes.'

'No.'

'Are you sure? Really sure?' With a jolt he started to rock the kayak from side to side. Faster and faster. Water seeped over the edges. His laughter turned pretend evil. 'You want to live dangerously?'

'Stop that!' She laughed as she hit the surface of the sea with the paddle again, hopefully soaking some sense into him. Nausea curled in her stomach. 'Stop.'

'Not until you say yes.' He rocked harder. Now water gushed in on one side.

'Stop, or you'll capsize us.' *And I'll lose my lunch.*

'Then I can save your life too and you'll be forever in my debt. Dashing hero opportunities abound. Say yes or you're getting an early bath.'

Laughing, she gripped the kayak as a mini-tsunami soaked her legs. 'No.'

'Yes!'

'Ohmygod, yes! If it shuts you up, yes!' The thought of spending an evening with him in a fancy dress appealed. At the plush Heritage Hotel too. God, how she'd love to walk in somewhere like that on his arm. But she wouldn't. She'd cry off later, once she'd explained. Right now land was in sight and she didn't want to have to swim the distance. 'Now, get me to that shore before I feed you to the plankton.'

The walk to the summit was planned to take an hour, but judging by the way she stumbled up-wards over loose black volcanic rock, Gabby thought it could take a lot longer. Getting pur-chase on the slippery path proved difficult and took more effort than she thought she had. The route took them deeper into thick bush, where they stopped only briefly to read signs telling the six-hundred-year history of the volcano.

Gabby hurried forward with the front group. Since coming ashore she'd managed to get herself nestled into the hustle and bustle of the climb and was grateful not to be on the edge with Max. She didn't trust herself to be alone with him. Before she knew it she'd be agreeing to much more than the awards dinner.

At a fork in the path an orange arrow signalled an alternate route taking them to the top via lava caves. She hesitated, wanting to see what these amazing-sounding formations must look like. But the rest of the group ploughed ahead, oblivious, the race foremost on their minds.

She watched their disappearing backs. 'Hang on! Does anyone want...?'

'I do.' Max's voice was like chocolate sauce over ice cream. Melting and thick. And hot.

'But you won't win the race.'

'Like I care.'

'You mean you would willingly lose?' Her hands found her hips. 'You're really letting the Maitland side down, there.'

He smiled. 'I think I already have my prize.'

Then he was reaching for her hand. Dragging her into the seclusion of one of the larger caves. It was cool and dark and smelt elemental—earthy, sensual. He pulled her in further, his hands circling her waist. Those all-blue Maitland eyes gazed down at her. God, he was divine. And hers for the taking if she wanted. All she had to do was breach that two-inch gap between them.

She struggled to get away. At least her head did. Her body glued itself to him.

He ran his tongue over her top lip, slowly. Achingly slowly. 'Kiss me.'

'What?' She pressed her hands against his chest, ready to push away. But her fingers curled into the fabric of his T-shirt as if making a stand. *We shall not be removed.* Excellent, just what she needed—renegade hands. 'Kiss you, here? You think that's wise?'

'It's the wisest thing I've ever done. Look…' He pointed to the thick shrubbery covering the view of the inside of the cave from outside. 'No one knows, no one cares. Hell, I'm sick of hiding out. I don't care who knows. And I'm going mad looking at the sway of your backside as you walk up that hill. I've got to kiss you. Now.'

'One kiss?' She could do that. One kiss. One final kiss. What harm would it do? 'Just one.'

'Or two, if you insist.'

'One is fine.'

'Yes, Charge Nurse Radley. And then I'll claim another later. And another. And another. When we're on our own. In bed.'

A tight fist clenched in the pit of her stomach. She wasn't being honest with him. She shouldn't be here doing this. But, God, she wanted to. Too much.

'No…listen, Max. We need to talk. We can't—'

Before she could find the right words his mouth lowered onto hers. Such a gentle pressure, sweet and soft, suckling her lip. The simple, perfect pleasure of tasting him. He could be so tender yet so strong. So brilliant and yet so endearingly silly, it made her heart ache.

His tongue danced a slow dance against hers, teasing, enticing. Making her yearn for more. His body told her how much he wanted her. His mouth told her how much he cared. And she hoped she answered him with her response—at least her body was honest.

She clung to him in the damp darkness, not wanting to let go. He was so powerfully addictive, took her to places that she'd never been to before. Made her heart sing a soft and hopeful song where before it had played a fractured lament.

For a few beautiful seconds she allowed herself to take what she craved. Before the dumb bass notes in her head told her this was all kinds of foolish.

Then she managed to find the strength she needed to take a step back, even though the space between them filled with a rush of air that made her feel cold and she wanted to nuzzle back into his heat.

This had to stop. Insane. Senseless.

She turned her back, ignoring his hurt and confused look. And shouted back to him in the lightest voice possible, 'Race you to the top!'

The roughly hewn path gave way to countless wooden steps, getting steeper and steeper. She began to think it'd never end, and he'd catch her up and ask her a zillion difficult questions. But suddenly a bright blue gap in the bushline announced her arrival at the summit.

'Wow. That was worth the effort,' she spluttered to one of the guides as she managed the final few metres. Her heart hammered hard in her chest and sweat ran in rivulets down her back.

There were three-sixty-degree views as far as she could see—across the ocean to the east, and to the west where the melting sun cast a warm orange glow over the city and harbour. And right in the middle the Sky Tower rose magnificently, dwarfing the other buildings, like a needle jabbing the darkening sky.

'Here, eat something, keep that energy up. You're going to need it later.' Winking at her, Max handed her a plastic plate of cheese and crackers from the backpack he'd lugged up the hill. 'For the kayak home, obviously.'

He seemed a little frayed perhaps but kept up the smile as he set out the rest of the picnic on one of the wooden seats that made up the hexagonal lookout. Hummus, chicken, potted salads. Delicious, if she'd had an appetite. And very cute that he'd brought enough for her, too. Food certainly wasn't top of her list today.

All around, happy faces munched and chatted, congratulated themselves on such a fun way to spend the afternoon, challenged each other to a race back down and across to the city. Someone proposed a toast, and champagne flowed into plastic flutes. 'To the Paediatric HDU, and friends.'

When she saluted them Gabby realised they

were all raising their glasses to her. A buzz ripped through her. Knowing they'd accepted her had tears stinging her eyes. She was fast developing a group of friends she'd begun to care about.

Since coming to Auckland she'd done things she'd never imagined possible with her restricted upbringing. Breaking those shackles had been such a relief, she'd invented a new persona for herself. One she liked. Finally.

It was sad, then, that she had to let the best part of her experiences go. But she'd always known forever wasn't something she could do—and not with a man like Max. She toasted them back, unable to drag her eyes away from his. So blue, fervent and vibrant. So trusting—that was there too. A first. So she really would have to be honest, as soon as they hit the mainland again.

The thought of that made her head pound more. Her stomach knots tightened. She tore her gaze away and focused on his apartment high-rise, where she'd finally come to life again. Then the Sky Tower, where she'd confirmed that life, with his guidance. Auckland was Max's city and she'd never think of it again without memories infused with him.

'Time to move off, everyone. Watch your step

as you go back down,' the guide warned, as they all began to pack up. 'It's slippery underfoot and the head torches only allow a limited view. Keep close.'

Gabby hung back to walk with Rachel.

Big mistake.

'So, you and Dr Make-You-Weep over there. What's the story? He's getting very cosy.' Rachel's tone was friendly and sincere. But it sent a rattle of nerves down Gabby's spine. She didn't want to become the subject of office gossip.

'Oh? You think so? I can't say I've noticed.'

'Come on. He can't keep his eyes off you. And you go gooey every time you look at him—like you're melting right there on the spot. It's pretty damned obvious there's a thing happening.'

'There's no thing.' Gabby's voice crackled. She tried to keep it steady as she whipped up the pace. With Rachel's probing questions and having lost sight of the others, she suddenly felt uncomfortable. They were falling behind. It was dark. And cold. And eerily quiet. 'Let's catch the others up. I don't want to get lost.'

'Wait. Hang on. Tell me about— Wait,' Rachel called. Then, 'Oomph…oww.'

There was a slight shiver in the air, the crackle

of breaking branches. A loud scream. A thump of bone versus wood.

'Rachel? Where've you gone? Are you okay?' Heart thumping against her ribcage, Gabby retraced her steps and shone the beam of her head torch onto the ground. Her friend had disappeared. *No.*

'Rachel? Rachel? Where the hell are you?'

This wasn't funny. The darkness covered everything like a thick black shroud. Gabby squinted and tried to scan the area but it was too dark, too hard to see anything beyond muted shapes and shadows. She managed to make out a steep bush-covered ravine dropping off the side of the path. Through broken foliage, way down, she made out a shape. Her heart beat a panicked tattoo in her chest. 'Rachel? Is that you? Are you okay?'

The shape groaned. 'I'm here,' Rach whimpered. 'My leg…hurts… I'm bleeding. A lot. Please. Help me.' Her voice wobbled and Gabby heard the beginnings of a sob.

Rachel was a competent nurse who wouldn't freak easily. Which meant things were serious. On a tiny uninhabited island. In the dark. And now left behind by the others.

Okay. Breathe. 'Hold on. I'll come and get you.'

'No.' Panic filled Rachel's voice. Panic, and pain. 'You won't manage, it's steep and dangerous. Get Rob. Max.'

'I'll come down first and check you out.' With her first step into thin air Gabby lost her balance, grabbed on to roots and earth and then nothing with her flailing arms. Tumbled over and over down the ravine, scratching her skin on sharp twigs. 'Whoa! This is lethal.'

Her arm hit against a spindly trunk and she grabbed it, held on with everything ounce of strength she had, tearing the skin of her palm to shreds. Bringing her catapulting body to a hard stop.

After a couple of seconds to catch her breath she pulled herself to standing and reassessed the situation.

Safety first—assess the environment. Should have done that before. 'Okay, Rach. Wait here. Don't move. I'm going to scramble up to the path and get the others. I'll be back as soon as I can.'

'Please hurry. Please.'

The pain in Rachel's voice spurred her up the slippery incline.

It was too dark and dangerous to run. The loose scoria slid under her weight and she had to concentrate on keeping upright. Stepping gingerly over the rubble, she called out to the others, trying not to sound like she felt. Lost and lonely, scared and hurting. 'Max. Max. Quick!'

In the distance she heard the low rumble of laughter.

'Max!' She called louder, unable to erase the panic from her voice. Kilometres of ocean stood between them and any proper medical help. And she still hadn't been able to assess her friend in any kind of way. A lot of blood, she'd said. Gabby didn't want to imagine the dark possibilities. But they were real. 'Max. Please. Please. Help me.'

The voices stopped. Then she heard a thunder of footsteps.

Never had she felt so relieved as when she saw his large shape hurtle towards her out of the gloom. He was a doctor. He'd be able to sort out her friend.

No. It was way more than that. Her heart lifted every damned time she set eyes on him.

When he reached her his hands gripped her shoulders as he scanned her up and down. 'What the hell…? Are you okay, Gabby? My God. You scared the living— You're okay?' Now he was holding her tight in his arms. His lips were pressing on her forehead. In front of the whole crowd.

Before she shoved away she committed the feeling to memory. His smell. The shape of him. The feel of him as his body fitted so perfectly to hers. One last time. Her throat closed over and she forced words out as she directed them to the damaged foliage and the drop. 'It's Rachel. She's down there. She's hurt her leg.'

And it's my fault. She shouldn't have hurried like that in the dark, shouldn't have made Rachel run to catch up just because she was avoiding a difficult topic of conversation. 'But be careful, Max. It's dangerous.' She wouldn't forgive herself if something happened to him, too.

Within seconds he was scrambling down the ravine, assessing the situation. After a few minutes his calm voice rose through the darkness. 'Hey, listen, I think Rach has an open fibula fracture. We're going to have to call the coastguard— there's no way she can kayak back. But I need a hand to get her out.'

Between them they scrambled together a wound dressing and fashioned a splint out of a walking pole. Then they carried Rachel down to the jetty and waited for help to arrive. Night clung to them, darker and colder, as they waited anxious minutes.

After what seemed an age, lights loomed out of the darkness and two paramedics jumped off a boat onto the jetty.

As they waved her off, Max grinned. 'She seems a lot better with Rob holding her hand. Job done.'

'Yeah. There's definitely something brewing there. I just wish it hadn't all ended like that.' Then she admitted the truth. 'It was my fault.'

'No, it wasn't.'

'I should have made us stay with the group.'

Instead of trying to avoid you. I should have been honest from the start, instead of trying to take what I wanted.

Greedy. Impetuous. Selfish. Nonna was right all along. One day you'll pay, my girl.

She'd been paying every day since.

With all the excitement, Gabby had forgotten her own unease. But now it came back with force. Her legs turned jellylike as her stomach stabbed and swirled. 'Please, can we go now? I'm so tired.'

'Hey, you're shaking. Here.' Taking off his fleece jacket, Max wrapped it round her shoulders. Despite his heat coating her limbs, she didn't think she'd ever be warm again. 'Too much excitement for one day, eh?'

Max held the kayak steady as she wobbled into it. Sitting down was the sweetest feeling she'd had for days. As she turned round to nod to him her vision didn't keep up with her head. Whoa. She needed to lie down. Now.

And she needed to find the right words to say to Max.

But her head was filled with cotton wool. And she was so cold she longed for strong arms to warm her. His arms. Please.

She began to shiver and had to focus hard on keeping the swaying paddling rhythm.

She barely noticed the lanterns the guide had attached to poles on the kayaks bobbing gently in the breeze, creating a magical soft glow across the jetty.

Barely felt the water spray her skin as Max powered the kayak towards the city.

Barely realised she had no strength of her own to even hold the paddle now that every ounce of energy had deserted her. Exhaustion finally oozed into her bones and made her feel cold. So very cold.

As she pulled the paddle towards her the pain

in her belly intensified like a bright, sharp knife, twisting and turning. Sharper. Hotter. Harder.

And suddenly she was falling into a black space... She tried to grab something, grasped for the paddle, at the water, at Max. Grabbed at nothing...

CHAPTER ELEVEN

'GABBY! GABBY!' MAX'S heart pumped into over-drive. She'd slumped to the side, her face skimming dangerously close to the water.

He couldn't get purchase on her, though he grasped at her. Tried to pull her upright. 'Gabby. Wake the hell up.'

After hauling in her fast-disappearing paddle, he took a huge breath and leaned towards her, cursing the damned lack of space.

If he leaned too far he'd capsize the kayak and have them both in the water.

A scenario he didn't want to contemplate.

'Gabby. Come on, girl.' He dragged her back by the shoulders and patted her cheeks, hoping his wet, cold fingers would jolt her awake. 'Couldn't you have done this when we had the coastguard out? Two rescues for the price of one? Hey, sweetheart. Wake up.'

Her face was white, her lips dry. Crap. Pushing her hair back, he found a pulse. Weak and fast.

She'd just fainted. But she wasn't regaining consciousness. This wasn't a regular thing. This was bad news.

'Hey! Hey!' Trying to get the attention of the other kayakers, he shouted. But the wind dragged his voice back out to sea.

The shore was tantalisingly close. A few hundred metres, maybe. He could get there in a matter of minutes. Raise the alarm.

Hauling in a breath, he infused every ounce of energy he had into getting her to that beach. His arms pumped until they burned. His lungs craved more and more oxygen but he was too focused on that shoreline to breathe.

After moments that seemed like forever he was kneeling next to her on the damp sand. Using his lifejacket as a pillow, he laid her down and bent her legs against his chest. 'Gabby. Come on, girl. Gabby.'

God. Think. Focus. What could it be? Just a vaso-vagal? But why?

'Max?' Her eyes fluttered open and she cradled her stomach protectively. 'It hurts so much...'

Then she was gone again.

He couldn't even get her focused enough to answer simple questions.

A few stragglers from the trip hovered around but he swatted them away. There was nothing for it. 'I'm taking her in.'

'Ambulance?' someone shouted above the concerned huddle. 'I'll call one now.'

Wait? For how long? Until she became critical? No way. He dampened down his tachycardia and worked out a plan. 'I'm not prepared to wait. I'll drive.'

Picking her up, he stalked over the sand and across the road to his parked car. Edged her gently onto the back seat and made sure to keep her legs raised to stimulate oxygen flow back to her brain.

That was when he noticed the blood.

God. No. What the hell...?

In all his years as a surgeon he'd never felt panic. Even when working on his nephew he'd had faith in his own capabilities. But right now, as adrenalin surged through him, his heart rate rocketed and he wanted her fixed. Immediately.

Thrusting the car into heavy traffic, he cursed loudly. Then he put his foot down.

Running the length of the hospital car park barefoot, fuelled by a need to save her, he finally got her to the emergency department. Faster than an ambulance could have made it. And he'd managed to keep some kind of observation going in the rear-view mirror. Resps: too fast. Pain: severe. She'd flicked in and out of consciousness.

He tried to keep his heart out of it. But, man, he couldn't. Couldn't reconcile the vivacious woman he knew with the damaged body in his arms. He would never leave her side again. Never.

When he ran in and saw Mitchell his heart beat faster. The best ER medic in town.

Thank God. And like Max himself, he would put everything aside to help his brother.

Now he knew what Mitch had felt like when he had agreed to do Jamie's surgery. Someone who had a vested interest—someone who'd care. He hoped. At least, if not for him then for Gabby. Mitch would repay the debt.

He managed to haul in air and relay her symptoms as they found a trolley and laid her on it. 'Weak, rapid pulse. Bleeding, I guess vaginally. She has severe pain in her abdomen.'

'Where?'

'Lower right side.' He tugged hard at his tumultuous memory. What had she said…? 'She mentioned something about her shoulder, too. Now I assume it could have been referred pain.' They'd put it down to the jolt of the SkyJump.

His hands fisted. Stupid. Damned stupid. They should have acted faster. He was a doctor. He should have known.

His eyes were drawn to the blood on her shorts. Thick. Dark. Too much. His stomach twisted and he beat back nausea.

Mitchell examined Gabby, talking gently, but she was too lost in pain to answer much. 'Her blood pressure's very low. I'll fix some fluids to bring it up. And I'll page the obstetrics reg.' He attached an oxygen mask, heart and blood saturation monitors. 'Any chance she could be pregnant?'

Holy hell. It had flitted through Max's head as a possible cause. But they'd used contraception the whole time. Condoms, and then the Pill. She'd been definitive about that, and said he'd been the first in a long time. Unless she'd been lying. 'I don't think so. But I guess technically she could be.'

'We'll run some tests. And do an ultrasound scan.'

'I'll come with her.'

'You'll get in the way, Max.'

'You take her anywhere without me and there'll

be trouble.' It was the first time he'd ever lost control. The first time he'd ever wanted to lay down his own life for someone else.

Gabby's eyes flicked open, searching around the room, and her frightened gaze fell on Max. She reached for his hand and held on as if her life depended on it. God, it just might if they didn't find the cause.

Hurry the hell up. 'Give her some pain relief first.'

His brother's palm fitted onto Max's shoulder. 'Max, it's okay. I know what I'm doing. I'll sort it.'

'Then do it.' He twisted out of his brother's grip and held Gabby's hand, brushed her thick curls from her face.

Damn her for not listening to him. Damn himself for not making sure she got checked out. It was his job to notice symptoms. But she'd been too caught up in making people happy, in putting herself at the bottom of the pecking order. And he'd been too caught up in letting her have her own way.

He ran his hands through his hair. 'Sort it now, Mitch.'

He wasn't prepared to lose her, not when he'd only just found her.

* * *

Five hours later, five damned hours, numbness ran through Max as he waited on a hard plastic chair outside Theatre Two. Okay, so he wasn't supposed to be here. But, what the hell, he had to be somewhere since they'd all but banned him from the OR.

Being a surgeon at least had some perks. They understood his panic. Cut him some slack. He drew the line at squinting through the blacked-out window, though. Couldn't bear to see her like that, lifeless and fragile. Because he knew he'd be in there otherwise, throwing his weight around and interfering in stuff he'd be better to leave alone.

A cup of weak hospital coffee was thrust under his nose. He took it, and when he looked up he was face to face with his mirror image. Only he knew he looked a damn sight worse right now. 'Thanks.'

'You okay?' Mitch sat down next to him.

It was comforting to have him here. Despite everything, there was a definite connection. Something that undercut the pain, something that went beyond the present and deep into a past that they both shared. Six years of the past where they'd been inseparable. So it was okay to be honest. 'Nah. Truth is, Mitch, I'm scared for her.'

'Truth is, you love her.'

Wow. That had come from nowhere. Did he? After such a short time? And how the hell did Mitch know?

Because Mitch had known everything, once. Whatever he himself wasn't, Mitch had made up for. A right and a left. Two halves that made way more than a whole. They didn't have that telepathy thing going but they did have some weird mutual understanding. 'I don't know if that's possible, Mitch.'

'I think you do.' Mitch bumped against him in a kind of friendly nudge. 'That's okay, you know. You can love someone.'

Max didn't want to. Had never wanted to, not if his emotions paid such a price. He'd been running on empty for so long. 'Can I? Can we? After everything that happened to us?'

'Well, I do. I love Jodi and Jamie more than anything. And it involves risk. You have to put yourself on the line. And God knows whether they're going to be here tomorrow—you and I both know the realities there. But it's worth every second you spend with them anyway.'

And that was about the most honest thing Mitch had said to him in nearly thirty years. Decades of pain welled up in Max's chest until he could barely breathe. 'But what happens if it falls apart? What if they…you know…?'

'What if they leave?' Mitch dragged his chair across the linoleum to face Max. 'Well, you'll survive. You will. You're strong. You're a Maitland, for God's sake.'

A Maitland. Brothers. Tied together by blood, the same DNA. Identical. But so many differences for so long.

Silence stretched across the gap between them, wound through the corridor, filled the spaces. And along with it came an immense need to talk to Mitch. Really talk. The way he'd wanted to since…since forever. 'I missed you like hell, you know. After they took me away.'

If he was surprised at this admission, Mitchell didn't let it show on his face. His gaze dropped to the paper cup in his hand. 'You didn't even look back. I thought you were glad to be leaving me behind.'

What? 'Glad?' It was so far from the truth it was laughable. Thick emotion filled Max's throat. Sucking in oxygen, he forced words out.

'Dumbass. I was your big brother. I was supposed to stop it happening, and I couldn't. It was bad enough that I failed you. I couldn't look back and let you see me cry, too. What would you think of me then?'

'That you cared.'

Holy hell. 'You thought I didn't care, Mitch?'

'I was six. I didn't exactly rationalise it. Everyone was leaving, and you didn't seem to kick up a fuss. Then there was all that competitive stuff. If it hadn't been for the spectre of your success, I'd have been happy. Especially since you didn't seem to care about me. I hated it, and in a screwed-up kind of logic ended up hating you too.' He paused. Breathed. 'And then there was Jodi…' Mitch's gaze hit him. Honest. Sincere. And filled with the same kind of feeling Max had churning round his gut. Something like an apology. A need to make things right. Mitch smiled. 'I love her. Honestly. I wasn't trying to play her. Or you. It wasn't a game to me.'

Max shrugged as he heard what he'd always known but had chosen not to believe. 'Yeah. I know that now. Didn't seem like that at the time, though.'

'Guess we need to grow up, right?'

'Yeah.' Taking a chance, Max stuck out his hand and Mitchell grabbed it. They hung on, way too long. Like two idiots.

Pretty momentous. This would be where girls hugged or something. They weren't there yet, but it was ground-breaking Maitland history.

Max's heart squeezed with relief. A stupid stinging sensation hit his eyes as he looked into his brother's. They dropped their hands. Looked away. At the floor. At their feet.

But Max noticed the smile on his brother's face was as broad as his own.

Another silence followed, this time a more friendly one.

Eventually Mitch leaned across. 'The other day, when you were talking about Fred, you mentioned something about *stuff* happening. You want…?' Turning his palms up, Mitch offered Max his chance to explain.

But Max had shared enough today. 'Nah.'

'You sure?'

'Yeah. Long time ago. Best forgotten.'

'Maybe one day, right?'

'Maybe.' Goddamn, would that lump in his throat go?

One day he'd tell his brother the truth about the regular beatings, the pressure he'd had to excel, how much he'd wanted to be part of Mitchell's family, how jealousy had eaten away at him and turned into hate.

But for now it was enough his brother had asked.

Suddenly Max had to walk. Find some space. Breathe. For so long he'd wanted to end that rift between them. To tell the truth, finally.

Yeah, the truth was he'd missed and loved his brother. And he wanted him back.

He wanted a family. More than anything.

And more than that, he wanted to share it with Gabby.

Gabby.

Max stood and shook out his tight muscles. Needed some air to unclog his throat. To think about his next step. 'Thanks, Mitch. Really. Thanks. I've got to go.'

'Anytime, mate. You know where I am.'

'Sure thing.'

Max walked out of the hospital, through the car park, over to the patients' garden, where he found a bench lit by a slither of moon.

Some joker had planted a peace sign made out of squat purple bushes, and a border of bright scarlet flowers. They reminded him of his sky garden. Of her. Of what she'd brought into his life.

Hell, everything reminded him of her. The Auckland skyline, sunshine. The hospital. His apartment. He looked at everything touched with her image or smell, or some memory.

He cared for her. That was the truth.

Love? He didn't know about that. Couldn't define it in such simple yet complex terms. But she was special. And he wanted her. Maybe they could agree to some sort of commitment. Make a first big step.

Even thinking about that word sent shivers running through him. This was so far out of his comfort zone he didn't know what to do. Say. Think. But he had a gut feeling they should try and take this to another level. He just had to wait out the hours it would take to fix her.

And while he sat it occurred to him that Mitch was way more evolved than he was. He had a girlfriend and a child. People he could share things with. To help him relearn the truth about love. And he wanted that so badly. With Mitch. With Gabby. Trouble was, he was scared. Because he knew that sometimes the truth hurt, too.

Finally the obs and gynae reg sauntered along the corridor as if he'd simply been to the park and not just saved a life. 'Hey, Max, she's out of surgery now. It was a bit of a mess really. Her right fallopian tube was just about to blow, so we removed it. But her left one is scarred too. She has grade-four endo.' The doc smiled gently and put his hand on Max's arm. 'I'm very sorry, but the chances of her getting pregnant naturally again are virtually impossible and very risky.'

Whoa. Hold on. This was too much to take in. Pregnancy? 'How far along was she?'

'Five, six weeks. We could talk about assisted fertility anytime you want. There are options.'

Endometriosis. Infertility. All added up to a bleak future. But she was safe and alive. And that's all he damned well cared about. 'No. Thanks. I don't need to talk about this right now. I need to see her.'

The doctor shrugged. 'Of course. When she's out of Recovery we'll take you up to the ward.'

'I'll walk her up from Recovery.'

'You and I both know that's not a good idea.'

Yeah, well, he hadn't had many of them recently.

She'd been pregnant. With his child. And had nearly died.

God. Clearly due to their recklessness. The Pill had failed, probably due to the vomiting bug they'd all had. He was surmising. Trying to make sense of it.

Had she known? He didn't think so. And now he had to tell her not only had she lost her baby but she couldn't have any more. Not without intervention. And there were never any promises there.

She didn't want kids—she'd told him that. And neither did he. He hadn't ever given it much thought on top of not settling down. Not having kids had completed that picture for him.

But this—this was a game-changer. Emotions he hadn't known he had seeped through his skin.

A baby. His baby. *A father.*

Wow.

No one had warned him about the intense possessiveness a man could feel just hearing a word. One simple word. And the crushing hopelessness. The heavy weight that pressed on your chest and stole your breath. The pumping of adrenalin. The way for a second the joy unfurled enough to create hope, before it was whipped away on a senseless, cruel wind of reality. A father no more.

Truth dawned, crystallised in front of him. He did want a family, to be a father, to give a child the kind of things he'd never had. It was a shock. It was too cruel to realise that now, when it was too late, that he wanted what Mitchell had.

Without giving a second glance to the doctor, Max stalked away.

His pacing outside the ward probably gave the nurses a scare but he didn't care. The second he saw them walking towards him he darted past and in to her bedside. She was all wrapped up in blankets and tubes. The regular beep of the monitors assured him that she was mending.

He took a seat next to the bed and held her hand until her eyelids fluttered open.

She blinked up at him with groggy eyes. 'Hey.'

A hot, unfamiliar feeling washed over him. Gratitude and relief mixed with that tight ache in his chest. She was safe but their baby wasn't. 'Hey. You gave us all a bit of a fright. We had to operate, but you're okay. And everything's going to be just fine.' He promised her that much. He'd make it right. Somehow.

'What was wrong? Appendix or something?'

He didn't answer directly, didn't want to upset her so soon after the surgery. 'Rest now, I'll explain it all later. You're doing great. How do you feel?'

She coughed and ran a palm over her dry lips. Her voice was crackly and hoarse from the intubation tube. 'On a scale of one to ten? Minus three. How do I look?'

'On a scale of one to ten? Eleven.'

'You are so full of—'

He squeezed her hand. 'Quiet now. The nurses said you weren't to get excited.' So how the hell he was going to tell her about the pregnancy and the scarring he didn't know.

Coward. She needed to know.

All in good time.

'Don't kid yourself, Maitland.' She managed a weak smile. 'You don't excite me. Irritate, obviously. Annoy, intensely.'

He couldn't help grinning. At least she hadn't lost her spirit. The one thing that kept her so beautiful, so different from everyone else. One of the many things he admired in her. 'They clearly didn't insert a "nice gene" while they were rummaging around in there.'

'Nice is so overrated.' As her eyes closed, her

breathing settled and her grip on his hand relaxed. 'I'm all out of talking. Now go.'

'Like hell. I'm staying all night.'

And then he'd broach the subject of the baby.

CHAPTER TWELVE

'THANK GOD FOR my own bed.' Gabby slunk further under her duvet and closed her eyes. Safe in her own space away from the prying eyes of the hospital staff. Without the cloying closeness of Max and his pitying looks. She needed space to grieve for the baby she hadn't even known had been growing inside her. To come to terms with it and, yes, to move on.

It felt like she'd be moving on forever. And yet she'd never escape.

She allowed herself a few moments to not think. To not do anything. The last hour had been so full of pain and arguments with the hospital staff. Now she just needed peace and quiet.

But half of her was on alert for the phone to ring. The doorbell. Her cellphone. Because as soon as Max found out he'd be on to her.

No matter.

He could go to hell like the rest of them.

Funny, though, there'd been no tears when the

nurse had whispered to her in the middle of the night and told her the truth of her situation. No tears, but a numbness that had spread through her body, a reconciliation that finally, *finally* Nonna's promised punishment had come.

No more babies. Nonna would be pleased up there on her fluffy perfect cloud—she'd warned something bad would happen. Now it had.

No babies.

For so long Gabby hadn't even wanted any more. Hadn't allowed herself to think of more. But now the ache in her stomach was nothing compared to the sharp hurt in her heart. Just like the first loss, this was devastating.

She did want children. She wanted to be a mother sometime. Somehow.

Each breath came coated with a stuttered pant. Everything she touched shook in her trembling hands. And yet there were no tears.

'Gabby. Gabriella!' A loud hammering on the front door jolted her upright.

Max.

She held her breath and waited for him to lose interest. Fat chance. The man was nothing if not determined. 'Gabby. Let me in. I know you're there.'

Pulling the curtains tight, she closed her eyes, wishing to hell she hadn't chosen a ground-floor bedroom.

'Gabby.' He'd moved now and was hammering on the French doors to her room. 'I'm going to break the glass if you don't answer.'

Protecting her abdominal wound with her arm, she dragged herself up and leaned back on her pillows. 'Go away, Max. Please.'

'I will not go away. Either you let me in or I break the glass. You want that to happen?'

No. She didn't want anything to happen. She wanted the world to stop. In fact, to rewind to that first night when she'd taken courage in both hands and walked back to his apartment. She liked that brave Gabby. She wanted to be her again.

Then she could change everything that had happened afterwards. Particularly the falling-for-him bit. And falling pregnant.

But there was no getting away from it, she had to face him. Face the world. She'd have to go back to work and he'd be there, too. At some point she'd need to look him in the eye and explain.

Because even though she'd long since reconciled the choice she'd made ten years ago, it was definitely the right one for them all. But she'd be taking a chance on Max believing her.

She edged carefully out of bed, opened the curtains and unlocked the latch. Might as well do it now. Be damned once and for all.

'Gabby, what the hell is going on? I leave the ward for an hour. One damned hour, and you discharge yourself. Are you okay?' His fierce gaze bored into her as he strode into the room. He scrutinised her, checked her, assessed her all in one look. And, yes, for the record, she felt wanting. Seemed her mojo these days was sneaking away.

She owed him an explanation, that much she knew. But did he have to break her heart all over again just by being so damned impassioned? And angry? And here?

He didn't deserve the pain he'd gone through, keeping vigil at her bedside. Or the inevitable pain she was storing up for him.

What she wanted was for him to climb right into bed next to her. What she wanted was to cling to him and never let go.

The right thing, however, was to be honest. And she was hardwired to do the right thing, no matter how much it hurt.

His lips formed a thin line and he looked utterly stunned. 'Are you barking mad?'

'No.' She eased back into bed. 'I just needed to get away.'

'How the hell are you going to look after yourself? What about your four-hourly obs, your medications?'

'I'm a nurse. I know what to do. I'll cope.' It wasn't the physical pain she was worried about.

He lifted the duvet and tucked her legs underneath it. Covered her up and took her pulse. Sat on the bed next to her. Only then did he lower his voice to somewhere around seething point. 'You want to tell me what's going on?'

She offered him a smile. 'Hospital food really sucks. I'm definitely going to have a meeting about that when I get back.'

'Food? Is that it? Really? You're crazier than I thought. I could have got you something, a takeaway. You should have said.' The concern on his face almost overwhelmed her. 'You look terrible.'

'Thanks. I feel like crap.'

'I wonder why? You are unbelievable.' She could see he was trying damned hard to be restrained when every impulse was to cart her back to the ward. The mad ward, probably. His breathing caught, and finally he snapped. 'Maybe if you'd stuck to doctor's orders, like any sensible person, you'd feel a little better. Maybe if you'd tried to talk to me instead of bottling it all up… What is it with you? When will you learn to talk to me? Tell me how you feel? When the hell will you trust me?'

I can't.

He started to gather up clothes from her armchair and stuff them into a backpack.

Jerking up, she tried to stop him. 'What are you doing?'

'I'm taking you back to the hospital until you're well enough for discharge. I will bring food in. Caviar, lobster or whatever the hell *Madame* requires. But you're going in.'

'No way. Put that down. Do not dare root through my stuff.' The pain finally winning, she sagged back against her pillow. 'We both know how desperate they are for beds. I'd be discharged tomorrow or the next day, anyway. I just need sleep.'

'And regular meds, and someone to cook for you.' He counted on his fingers before shaking his head in dismay. 'And someone to help you.

To care for you. That anaesthetic has done weird things to your brain.'

'I'm fine, but you're not listening. I want to stay here.'

'Okay, then, you win. I'll move in here and look after you.' He threw the bag to the floor. 'Do not argue about this.'

'No, Max, you can't move in, and I'm not going anywhere.'

'So I have to stand back and let you put yourself at risk? I'm your…what am I exactly? Your boy-friend? No. Your lover? Your confidant? I don't think so, because that would involve talking to me about things. You're clearly not safe to make any kind of rational decisions.' His face closed in and he stared at her. Then he actually laughed, deflating the tension. 'Unless it's to kiss me, of course. In which case I'd say you were very sane indeed.'

She turned her head away. 'No, Max. Please. Don't.'

The laugh turned bitter. 'I need to hold you, Gabby. I need to feel you in my arms. We both lost that baby. I know you're hurting. Hell, I'm hurting too.'

She knew that.

He'd come a long way. He could admit that he hurt. But she was still back in the emotional dark ages.

He hurt. For himself. For her. For what they'd lost.

Her throat clogged with thick emotion. She'd been thinking purely about herself and not how he felt about losing a baby, too.

What had happened to her? Had she always been so selfish? For so long she'd learnt to keep her emotions tightly locked away. Refused to discuss how she felt. Refused, even, to acknowledge that she felt anything at all. But now it wasn't just about her, it was about Max, too.

Her hand found his. 'I'm so sorry, Max. I know you'll make a great dad one day.'

'And you'll be a fabulous mum, somehow. But don't beat yourself up about it now. We can talk about all that another time. Just work on getting better.' His arm slid under her back and he pulled her to him. She knew he needed her comfort as much as she needed his. But she couldn't do this anymore.

'I can't hold you, Max. Not now.' Because if she did, she might never let go. 'Please, don't.'

Confusion shimmered in his eyes. 'When you're ready, let me know.'

He pulled his arm away but stayed on the bed next to her. A gap of a few inches separated them. Judging by the frustration emanating from him, it might as well have been a mile. An ocean. A continent.

Minutes ticked by. His breathing settled but he wasn't relaxed, not by a long shot. His thigh muscles remained tight under his jeans, his fists clenched at his sides.

It took all her strength not to reach for him.

Eventually he shifted from the bed. 'I'm going to get some food for you. Don't you dare move before I get back—I can't keep chasing you across the city. Besides, I want you strong and well for that dinner next week. I want to show you off.'

She knew he meant well and was trying to give her a focus to distract her. A reason to heal. Well, she didn't want one. She didn't want to be looked at and pitied. And she didn't want to string him along anymore. She needed to set him free. 'I'm not going to the dinner.'

'But you said—'

'I know what I said. But I have to tell you something.' She drew in a breath and readied herself for the most painful conversation of her life. 'I can't go—'

'Of course you can.' He spoke over her. Goddamn him. 'You'll be fine by then. You need something to look forward to. Is it because you have nothing to wear?' He'd jumped off the bed and walked across the room towards her closet. 'Let's see what you have in here.'

'No! Max, stop. Listen to me.' She leaped forward but a sharp sting across her incision scars whipped her breath away.

Before she could stop him he'd opened the closet door. He reeled back. 'Oh, okay. Wow. You have a lot of shoes. And so neatly stacked. You have OCD, too?'

No. No. No. Everything was unravelling exactly the way she didn't want.

She wanted to scream. To run.

'Don't…touch the boxes.' *Please, don't. Please, don't. Please, don't.* 'Max, come away from there.'

'Hey, silly. It's just shoes.' He picked up box three and examined it. His forehead furrowed as he took in the childish train stickers. The blue balloons. The number three in navy and silver glitter. 'What are the numbers for? You rating your shoes now, too?'

'Max—no.'

His hands were opening the lid. Her heart thumped and pounded and rattled. Her shoulders hunched up and squeezed against her neck. *Don't. Don't. Don't.* She closed her eyes. Opened them again to see the nightmare had become a reality.

He would ask. She would have to tell him. It would be over.

'What's all this, Gabby? I don't understand.' His voice was hollow as he showed her the contents of the box. Contents she'd painstakingly put there. The birthday card so lovingly written, that one day she hoped she'd be able to give. The carefully selected presents. The letters. 'What's this about?'

Her hand found her mouth and stopped the wobbling lip. But she couldn't stop the tears that threatened and yet never fell. Somehow she forced the words out through her burning throat. 'They are for my baby.'

Pain crawled across her stomach, up her spine, reached out to her fingertips, down her legs to her toes. Every part of her burned with the loss.

'Your what?' His focus was back on the boxes, his voice empty.

'There are ten of them. One for each year he's been alive. One for every birthday I've missed.'

Again he shook the box towards her. 'I don't understand. What are you telling me?'

'You'll get the chance to be a father again and again, Max. But I won't ever be a mother. Not again. I was once, though.' Now her heart shattered into a million tiny jagged pieces that would never fit back together again. She'd lost everything. She'd lost her babies. She watched as he recoiled, his face a grim mask of disgust. And now she was losing him, too. She was utterly broken. 'I gave my baby away.'

He couldn't believe what he was hearing. What did she mean? Gave it away? 'I don't understand.'

Didn't want to comprehend what she'd done. He gazed at the neatly stacked numbered boxes. One to ten. Covered in a pathetic collection of stickers that were aged appropriately. From teddy bears, bubbles and balloons to music players and groovy cartoon kids on skateboards. They looked like collages done by a child. The sense of hopelessness that accompanied them was almost palpable. And mirrored the same feeling he had in his soul.

Her eyes were dead. Her face a mask. How she held herself together to say those words he'd never know. But he needed to hear the rest. To discover what kind of person he'd lost his heart to. Because, God knew, she wasn't the woman he'd believed her to be. 'Go on, Gabby. I'm listening.'

Her voice, in contrast to his hoarseness and harshness, was shallow and soft. He had to strain to hear her. And yet he couldn't bring himself to move closer.

She gripped the necklace at her throat. 'I fell pregnant when I was fifteen. First time lucky.' The smile was false. 'First and only time. Until you.'

He supposed that should mean something. She'd waited how long to put her faith in someone? And she'd chosen him. But it didn't change anything. Couldn't change what she'd done. She'd given a baby away…for adoption? Foster care?

The same kind of life he'd had.

But it wasn't the same, he tried to rationalize. This was his Gabby, beautiful, kind Gabby who wanted every baby to be loved and looked after. She'd drilled that into him enough already. He couldn't imagine her doing such a thing.

So why? Why had she given a baby away?

Had she no idea how that kind of stuff messed with your head? How it always felt like rejection? At least, that's what he'd always felt. Like he was something nobody had wanted. Not his parents. Not his brother. Certainly not his uncle.

Rational thoughts twisted and screwed in his head. God, he was all kinds of confused.

He watched her throat rise and fall against the diamond heart as she picked her words. He couldn't find any words of his own so he let her purge herself.

She didn't look at him. Instead, she spoke to the space between them, her gaze directed somewhere around his chest. 'I didn't realise I was pregnant until I was quite far along. Twenty weeks. I've always had irregular periods and everything seemed normal, until they stopped altogether. My mum went hysterical when I told her. We had no money, nothing, no way of bringing up another child. Eventually Nonna found out. She was furious. She'd spent her life bringing up my mum then me. She had no intention of doing it again, and definitely no inclination to help me. "Get rid of it," she said. "Otherwise everyone will look down on us even more. You don't bring dishonour on your family."'

His laugh was filled with scorn but he couldn't hold it back. 'What? In twenty-first-century New Zealand?'

'You know what it's like to be a pregnant school-girl, do you? How it is to be under the thumb of an über-strict family who are old-fashioned and proud, who would never ask for handouts. Nonna dictated everything. What I did, who with. She had control down to a T. She'd always said my mum had been out of control and that's why my father had left, so she wasn't going to risk it with me. Short of locking me in the house, she had a hand in everything I did, who I saw, where I went. Monitoring calls, checking my texts. It was worse than prison.'

And worse, then, than his uncle. Who hadn't cared what Max had done, as long as he'd excelled at it. Or had taken a beating.

'So this was the ultimate disgrace. Nonna threatened me. Told me I'd let the family down, that they'd disown me. Told me I was stupid and that I'd fail. That I'd be a useless parent, like my mum. That I would condemn my child to a life of poverty and misery, like mine.'

'And you believed her?'

'Truthfully? I was frightened to death of Nonna. She never hurt me physically, although she threatened it enough, but she was scathing with her tongue. She could twist anything to make you feel guilty and useless. "You'll ruin us, Gabriella. It's your fault we live like this, with next to nothing. Your fault we have no money. Do you know how much school costs? Food? Clothes? Bus fares? And for what? A stupid, selfish, hateful child who brings shame on us. You have the devil in you, Gabriella.'"

Gabby dragged in a breath, shoulders slumped forward, as if she still believed every word her grandmother had said. '*Hateful. Stupid. Selfish.* Emotional scars aren't so easy to see, right?'

'Right.' If what he was hearing was true, her scars ran as deeply as his. He knew exactly how she felt. But still… Giving a child away? Max tried hard to understand what she'd been through, but how to do that with a series of disconnected thoughts running through your brain?

Social workers. Screaming. *Dip dip dip.* Choices made, so much lost to him. And now his pain was heightened by the crushingly sad look in her eyes.

She sighed. 'I was naive, God knows. I wouldn't have got pregnant if I hadn't been. But I believed Nonna. Believed I was stupid. I believed I'd fail.'

But there had been two people responsible for this baby. It wasn't just about how well Gabby would have coped.

'What about the father? Didn't he care that you gave his baby away?' Because *he* would have cared. He'd have fought for his child, whatever feelings he'd had for the mother. He wouldn't have given it away as if it were unwanted trash.

Gabby hauled in air. Just looking at Max's dark eyes destroyed her. She'd already lost him, that was obvious. Lost him because of something he'd never understand. But now that she'd started, she had to tell him the utter, absolute truth.

'Isaac was the only thing that made me feel I was lovable, desirable. Worth something. He was my guilty secret. In a family where I wasn't allowed any kind of normal social life, sneaking out to see him was my bliss.'

How naive and stupid she'd been. She'd truly believed the local college boy had been as committed as she had been. Blindsided by immature infatuation she'd thought was love, she'd been crushed when he'd rejected her. Risking that kind of betrayal again had been something she'd avoided for ten years. It hurt too much. Now, seeing the incomprehension in Max's eyes, the disgust and the anger, she decided she'd been right. 'When I told him we were having a baby he disowned me. He told me I was nothing to him. *Nothing.*'

Just like Max had. Nothing important.

The dark look she knew she threw at Max was jumbled with the mixed-up emotions of now and the past. She'd been so alone and scared, and rejected by everyone. But had made the very best decision she could at the time.

'Isaac didn't want a baby and told me to get rid of it. No one cared what I wanted, they just wanted the problem gone. Nonna arranged for me to move across Wellington to stay with a distant cousin until I gave birth. I was fifteen, Max, still a child myself. I couldn't imagine looking after a baby on my own, with no support. I couldn't do it.'

'There are social services. They'd have set you up in a flat.'

Oh, yes, he had all the answers. 'Easy in hindsight when you're a smart, rich doctor, but not when you're a scared teenager. Where would I have found out about that stuff? I was terrified. Terrified of giving birth, of being a mum, of being on my own. One night I was in the kitchen fighting with Nonna, and I suddenly saw everything clearly. I loved my baby so much I wouldn't let it eke out an existence like I had, where there was little love and too much control. My child deserved better than I could give him. I had nothing to offer. Certainly not a good life with a loving family. The kind of family I'd always dreamed of having.'

She nodded at Max as he dropped the box onto the floor and walked to the other side of the room. 'The kind you dreamed of too, eh? I didn't know what to do with a baby.'

'You can learn. There are books.' His jaw tensed and his lip curled. God, he really did hate her.

But she actually felt lighter by telling him. She was utterly broken but open. She'd never ever told anyone else about this.

'Nonna arranged a meeting with a private adoption agency who gave me files on couples who wanted a baby of their own. I chose one couple who sounded nice. But they were celebrities, the document said. They were desperate and they wanted a closed adoption to keep things from getting to the press. I realised, in the end, that was probably my best option. I wouldn't be able to watch someone else love him. It would break my heart to visit but not be able to have him with me. And I would never take him away from them, so they convinced me to give him up as quickly as possible, as it was best for all concerned.'

He leaned on the back of a chair, watched her from a distance, his gaze damning. And said nothing. She looked for a glimmer of understanding, but there was nothing but a taut stance and tight fists.

'In the hospital I held him for a few lovely hours. It was just me and him. I held him tight and told him over and over how much I loved him, how I wanted him to be strong and kind and happy. How proud I was of him already.' *How I was so, so sorry, but it truly was for the best. That I loved him so much I had to give him away.* There had simply been no other choice. The only way to be the best mum had been to give him to someone who could provide more than she ever could have.

Her lips wouldn't stop trembling. She bit them together. Tried to control herself. Relaxed her shoulders and finally let out the pain that had haunted her for a decade, and that she knew she would never shake.

'He was perfect, Max. So tiny. So beautiful. I gave him his own name, his name for a day: Joseph. My baby, Joe. I sang him a lullaby. Wrapped him in a blanket I'd bought—it's in box zero if you really need to know—just so I could have his smell with me for a bit longer. I spent those last minutes with him looking over his features, his tiny body, his little snub nose, at those teeny little fingernails. So I would never forget how he looked, what he felt like. So I would have something of his to remember him always. Just a snapshot in my head, but it's as clear today as it was then.'

How she would say the next words she didn't know. But she had to. She inhaled deeply and stilled the shaking in her voice. The bright ball of pain in her throat burned and prickled and throbbed. 'I pressed my lips to his perfect mouth and kissed him, and he gurgled. His baby voice was like sunshine, I didn't know he would sound so beautiful. I didn't know it was possible to feel so much love for someone I'd only just met.

'But then they came, and I told him again over and over how much I loved him. I loved him, Max. I hadn't got to know him, but it was there already, this immense and overpowering feeling for him. I loved him so much. That was all there was for me—my love for him. There was nothing else. Nothing. And then they came, and I handed him over. It was like a light going out in my soul.'

Just like that. Hers for a few moments, then gone. She hadn't known how she'd be able to live without him. How she could get up each morning and face a less bright day. But she had, believing he deserved better than what she'd had to give. Believing he was in a happier place.

But even then she'd wavered. Wondered if he was happy. Wondered if his new family burned with the same fervent love she did.

Wished she could turn the clock back.

And now she had nothing to look forward to. No child to hold in her arms. She ached as much for the baby she'd just lost as for the one she'd given away.

Tears pricked at her eyes but still none fell. Her throat was hoarse with an ache that she didn't think would ever heal, and the hole in her heart gaped wide.

'It was like a tight fist of pain that gets bigger and bigger until you think you're going to die because of it. For a long, long time afterwards I didn't get out of bed. I couldn't face each day. I wanted him back so much. I knew I'd made the right choice, but it was so hard to deal with. I loved him. I always will. And one day I'm going to see him again. Somehow.'

* * *

Max couldn't get past 'handed him over'. Handed him over like an unwanted Christmas gift.

He knew he should feel sorry for her, knew she couldn't have made any decision like that easily—but, damn, he couldn't stop his anger pouring out.

'If I ever had a child I'd keep it so close, treasure it. I wouldn't trade it away for a better future.' Or leave it behind like his parents had. He felt the rage spread across his chest. Rage for what? Now? Then?

He didn't know. But he heard it in his voice. Raw. Loud. 'You could have tried, Gabby, but instead you just took the easy route so you could carry on your life and be a success in your cosy nursing career. You are not the woman I thought you were.'

'Shut up. Just shut the hell up.' Her face darkened as she held up her shaking palm. Her voice rose a notch, coated with anger that matched his. 'You have no idea what I went through. You won't even listen, you're too caught up in your own drama. You make Joe sound like an inconvenience, not a baby.'

'Wasn't he?' Hadn't *he* been? He and Mitchell?

'No. No. No. And you make me sound uncaring and unloving, and I'm far from that.' Her finger pointed at him accusingly. 'I honestly thought you knew me better.'

'So did I, Gabby. So did I.'

'Seems we were both wrong, then. This is exactly what I didn't want from you. I thought, hoped, you might understand. I work hard every day so that when I do meet him, he'll be proud of what I've achieved. And I'll be able to hold my head up high and be someone he can respect. He might understand—more than you, it seems—why I did what I did.

'My life has never been "cosy". Everywhere I went in Wellington I bumped into people who knew me when I was pregnant and who asked what had happened to my child. You can't live four months in a place and not make some contacts. Sometimes they'd come into the ward. They'd ask difficult questions and then everyone I worked with wanted to know about it. And then there was the constant nagging from Nonna, and my mum. "Don't get into more trouble. You've ruined our lives".'

'Because you didn't become a doctor after that, and save their precious skins. I get it now.' The missing pieces slotted into place, making up an ugly whole.

Her voice rose even more. 'I couldn't eat or study for a long time. It was intolerable being around them, but they made me stay and make it up to them. I couldn't get away from it. And then—worse, much worse—every baby I saw, every child I looked after at work, I thought it might be him. My baby.'

'Not *your* baby. You gave up that right when you gave him away.'

She glared at him, eyes sparking with defiance. 'How dare you?'

'Don't like the truth?' He walked towards the door, but she was already out of bed and hobbling towards him, holding her side as she covered the distance. Her flimsy pyjamas barely covered the curves he loved. Her eyes sparked as anger took her too. Now he saw what had kept her going, what had been her salvation. She had spirit and hope and fight. She truly believed what she'd done had been for the best.

And, goddamn him, that was when he realised Mitch was right. He did love her.

Had loved her.

It was like a swift low blow to his chest. Something he had been avoiding all his life—giving his heart to someone else. But it had happened. He'd given it to the one person he should never have fallen in love with, but he'd done it anyway. And he'd been right, all along, too—the truth hurt, but love hurt more.

Right now he didn't know what to feel. He didn't want the kind of bleak future it would be without her. But he couldn't see a future that involved someone so careless about life, about a baby—no matter how much she told him she'd given her child up in an act of love.

And he'd had to wring it out of her. 'What kind of a relationship is built on silences and lies? Would you ever have told me this if you hadn't had the pregnancy?'

At the word 'pregnancy' she flinched. He felt the sudden stab in his heart, too. Truth was, it all hurt much more than he cared to admit.

'We didn't *have* a relationship, Max. To be honest, we don't know how. We're both too damned scared.' She stopped short in front of him, huge, furious eyes boring into his soul.

Although he was tempted to fling everything he had at her, he would never tell her how much he had grown to like her. To love her. And how much her story mingled with his hurt and made everything sour.

She shook her head, her eyes glistening with unshed tears. It damn near broke his heart. But he couldn't touch her now, not after this.

'I don't know if I'd ever have told you. I wanted to but I didn't know how. Seems I was right—just look at your reaction.'

'Did you ever trust me?'

She blinked then turned away. 'I don't know that either.'

'Did you even try?'

'I don't—'

'You don't know. You don't know. Yeah, I get it.' He huffed out an angry breath. 'Seems to me you don't know a great deal, Gabby. Except, of course, about hiding the truth.'

'Yes, and opening up has done me a fat lot of good.' She pushed her fists into his chest. 'In an act of love I gave him a better chance at life. But you just don't want to understand.'

'Oh, I do, Gabby. I understand entirely.' He lifted her hands away from his body and dropped them by her sides, didn't want her touch on his skin. 'I think your baby was inconvenient. I know all about that because that's what we were to my parents. That's why they dumped us with a nanny while they went off on their nice little sailing trip. I know what it's like to play dip, dip, bloody dip, too. And to lose. To be given to people who turn out not to be the loving family you deserve. I know exactly what it's like to be unwanted.'

'Oh, I wanted him, Max. More than anything. But you don't always get what you want, right? Like this. Us. I wanted you. For the first time in forever I thought I'd found someone I could fall in love with. I wanted us to make a go of things. But not now. Not when you won't even try to put yourself in my shoes. You're just like Nonna and Mum, you think I'm completely selfish too.' He saw the torrent of fury swell through her, watched her try to stay in control but fail. She jabbed her finger into his chest. 'You are way out of line, mate. The far bloody side. Don't dare judge me. Don't. Ever. Judge. Me.'

He held her gaze, saw the tumult of emotions there, the rage, the sadness simmering through her. The dying hope. Felt it reverberate through him. A black mist coated everything he saw— hopeless and livid.

Shoulders lifting, she shook her head and stalked to the door. 'Now, I've got a lot to work through, and you're not helping at all. In fact, you're making things a whole lot worse. So you'd better go.' She waved her hand as if he was some insignificant interference. 'Just go. And don't even think about coming back.'

In truth, he knew it was for the best. It was over. Messy and painful. But over. 'Don't worry, Gabby. I'm out of here.'

And with that he turned around and walked out of her life.

CHAPTER THIRTEEN

THERE WAS NO getting back from this, Gabby knew.

Max had gone because of decisions she'd made when she'd been a child. But she understood how he'd see her now—as a woman who had committed the most heinous sin in his book.

So she couldn't blame him. She could run after him, try to explain, pound her fists against that bruised heart of his. But it would do no good. She knew enough from the bleak expression on his face that there truly was no going back.

Great, Nonna. Happy now? The punishment was cruel but deserved. She'd lost two babies, her fertility, and the man she loved.

Her breath stuttered as she scraped in air. Yes. The man she loved.

From the first moment he'd offered her those cheesy chat-up lines she'd fallen for him, too fast. Gabby, who shunned any contact with men, who focused entirely on her career, who never allowed so much as a flutter of her heart, had given him a huge piece of it that she would never get back.

Could it get any worse?

Oh, yes. Even more cruel, she'd have to face Max every day at work. Stand next to him as they worked on a patient together. Offer him a confident smile during a ward round. Be the ultimate efficient nurse she'd trained herself to be. Not wince at the rumours or the reality of him seeing someone else, settling down. Because he deserved that, at the very least. After what he'd been through he deserved a chance to be happy.

She'd made a huge decision to give up her baby, but seeing how damaged Max had been, being brought up by people who hadn't wanted him, she was doubly glad she'd given Joe to a family who *had* desperately wanted him.

She instinctively knew her son was safe and happy. Without her.

Now she had to prove she could still live without him. And without Max. No matter how hard it was, no matter how much hurt and pain she suffered.

But she would manage that, too. The one thing Max had given her was faith in herself, a renewed vision of life as something to celebrate, not hide behind.

Jumping off that tower had been the beginning, and now she would take every moment and grasp it. So she could show them all, show Max, show Joe, show Nonna—*show herself*—that she would never be beaten. She would fall, sure, but she would get up and keep going.

The ache in Gabby's throat burned fiercely as she replaced the lids on the boxes and stacked them in order back in her closet. Tempted for a moment to haul out Joe's blanket and press her face into it in search of a smell long lost, she instead found the steel in her back and fitted the lid tightly.

Pressing a kiss on her fingertips, she placed them on top of the box and then closed the cupboard door. She would continue to buy gifts for her precious boy, would write him those letters, but she would now reassert her own future. After all, that was why she'd come to Auckland in the first place.

She would not have a family, the one thing she'd wanted most but had been too afraid to admit. She would never hold her own baby in her arms again. She would never curl into Max's heat and let him soothe away the stress of the day. Or share a smile with him. A meal. A bed. But she would survive. Just. She had before.

Even though her heart was breaking all over again.

She looked over to where Max had tried to hold her in bed. To the door still swinging on its hinges with the force of his exit. Breathed in the last remnants of his smell.

He was gone. The sad story of her life.

Her bottom lip wobbled and she could feel her renewed determination wavering. She would allow herself one day to grieve, then she would forge forward.

Crossing the bedroom floor, the pain in her abdomen returned, accompanied by the familiar dull throb of regret. She climbed back into bed and pulled the duvet up to her chin.

Only then did she feel the dampness on her cheeks. When she glanced down she saw the droplets on her top.

And at last let the tears flow.

'A load of fuss over nothing. It's just a pompous dinner.' Max flicked Jodi's hand away as she fiddled with his bow tie. After his heart to heart with

Mitchell, everyone had relaxed. Even Jodi. Gone was the nervousness, the awkward glances, and into their place had slipped a gentle burgeoning friendship.

The rest of the guests had started to filter into the opulent Heritage Grand Tearoom. Jodi tutted. 'And it's an award. For you. You've at least got to have a straight bow tie in the photos.' She shook her head. 'You're like a bear with a sore head these days, Max.'

'I'm busy. Too busy for this kind of thing.' And he was. Since they'd lost their baby, and Gabby had dropped the adoption bombshell, he'd buried himself in work, too numb to contemplate a next step.

'Max, really?' Jodi's eyebrows raised. 'For as long as I've known you, you've never been too busy for praise. In an ego contest, you and Mitch would tie for first place. And then coerce the poor judges to decide on an overall winner. Then you'd argue about that, too.'

'So we've come a long way.'

'Yes, yes, you have.' She stepped back and admired her handiwork. 'I'm proud of you both.'

Mitch appeared and stuck out his hand. 'Hey. Time to go in? You ready?'

Max took his brother's offered hand and shook it warmly. 'Looks like I've been placed at your table. Is that okay?'

'No problem. Shame you couldn't have found a plus-one, though.' Mitch's voice was playful with gentle teasing, not the goading of the past. 'I mean, Max Maitland without a date? My, my! What is the world coming to?'

'Flying solo feels good right now.' Who knew? If he said it enough he might actually believe it. A part of him was missing. The best part.

'You mean she turned you down, right?' Mitchell laughed. 'What happened? You stuffed up again?'

'Yeah, well, with you all happied up, someone has to keep the family tradition going.' They shared a knowing smile. At least some things were improving, his family life if not his love life. That he could even be here with these two meant they'd made huge strides.

But Jodi wouldn't let it drop, even when they took their places at the plushly decorated table. She leaned across the crystal and glass and whispered, 'It's not healthy to work so hard, Max. You need some down-time. Get out there and play the field like you used to. God help me for saying this, but meet a girl, a different girl, have sex.' She patted Mitch's arm and smiled. 'Have some fun. It works wonders.'

'I don't want sex,' Max whispered in a gruff voice. At least, not random sex. He wanted sex with Gabby. And that was not going to happen anytime soon. Or ever. He'd drawn the line under that disaster and moved on.

He had.

If only he could stop stupid things reminding him of her. Like the ridiculous Sky Tower that invaded his vision every time he opened his curtains. The Shed. Mojitos. His bedroom. His damned annoying migraine-inducing scarlet sky-garden.

And right now the empty chair to his left was the most stark reminder of all that was missing from his life.

One week and it wasn't getting any easier. Yeah, he missed her.

Plain and simple. And way too complicated, just like everything that made up Gabby.

But he missed her.

Missed her sarcastic comments. The frowns. Her cute laugh. The feel of her. The tight press of her body against his.

Work had been almost intolerable. At first he'd missed her not being there. But, then, when she'd returned, he'd just ached to touch her.

But she'd broken his trust and he couldn't get past what she'd done. Couldn't fathom it. Given a child away. Hell, was there any worse thing to do?

She'd dented his stupid fragile heart. And he hated it.

He glanced around the room at the female guests swishing around in taffeta and silk. Once he'd have welcomed this kind of affair as a challenge: so many women, so little time. But tonight he just wanted to be on his own.

No matter. It was a temporary blip. In a few weeks or months he'd get back on the dating scene, wouldn't he? Go back to how things had been before he'd met her.

Was that possible? He couldn't remember the person he had been before Gabby had come into his life. He certainly didn't much like the man he'd been: an empty shell not prepared to feel anything. She'd made him want things: a commitment; a family; to finally fix things with his brother. And had given him the tools and courage to make them happen.

And now he'd let her go. But it had been the only sane thing to do. He just had to believe it.

After a passable dinner and a couple glasses of red wine, Max stretched his legs under the table and watched his brother and Jodi chat together.

The Jodi thing was definitely a pale memory. Just seeing them finish each other's sentences, the genuine warmth between them convinced him that what they had was forever. With Jamie well on the way to recovery and their relationship on track, he couldn't help admit that he was jealous. But, then, they'd gone through hell to get here, and Mitch had fought for his family every step of the way. Max didn't know if he'd have the strength to do that.

The MC called for silence and a few awards were dished out. Hating the phoney reverence and the limelight, Max cringed at the prospect of having to receive his. Was it too late to leave?

He didn't deserve an award for doing a job he loved. He just liked being able to give patients a second chance—surely everyone deserved one of those. He liked the satisfaction from a good day's work and coming home to… Damn, there was that reminder again. An empty flat.

'I'd now like to call upon the nominator of the

award for delivering excellence, Mitchell Maitland, to say a few words.'

'What?' Max stared at his brother. 'You nominated me? What the hell?'

'You saved my boy's life. Got to get my own back somehow.' Mitch stood and squeezed past, his grin broadening.

'God, no, Mitch—don't you say anything. They'll throw rotten tomatoes at me.'

'Ach, so you see through my dastardly plan.' Mitchell took to the stage, his tie perfectly straight, courtesy of his girlfriend. He cleared his throat and began his speech, his eyes fixed on Max.

'Max Maitland has brought many changes to the transplant service over the years. He's shaken it up, modernised it and even ruffled a few beaurocratic feathers, in true Maitland style. But now we have a service second to none in the OCD. Full credit to him. And, yes, I admit, we've had a few professional differences in our lives and a few personal ones, so some of you may be surprised I'm up here at all.'

He paused until the laughter died down. Looking around the room, Max realised how much their feuding had resonated across the hospital as a few of his colleagues nodded, but raised their glasses to Max and smiled. Seemed the whole staff body felt the effects of this Maitland thaw.

Mitch continued, 'As most of you are aware, things haven't been easy between us. But despite personal setbacks and challenges, Max has never been afraid to chase a dream, however hard it may seem, to do the right thing, to make countless people's lives better. Including my son's. And mine. And for that I can't thank him enough. In all my life I've never known a better man. So there is no more deserving recipient of this award, and I'm proud to call him my brother. I give you Max Maitland, recipient of the Auckland Hospital Delivering Excellence Award.'

After collecting the award, Max returned to the table and sat next to Mitchell. 'Whoa. That was unexpected. Thanks. Nice speech—if you can see through the bull.'

'Yeah, well, don't let it go to your head. And I expect at least three nominations in return from you next year. Between the two of us we could take this whole awards dinner out. What do you think—a Maitland coup?'

Max laughed. 'Think big, my boy. Next stop world domination. But we won't achieve that without working together. So how about we finally put the past behind us and look forward?'

Mitchell's jaw tightened as he thought about it, running his hand across his chin. 'We've been through a lot, you and me. What they did was wrong. No one asked us what we wanted, no one thought about what was best for us. We were too young to be heard.'

And neither of them had really recovered. At least, Max knew he hadn't. He was still stuck in the emotional wringer. Hence his accusations of selfishness and God knew what to Gabby. It suddenly became clear. He'd seen her actions through the tarnished lens of his own experiences, mixed up his issues with hers, and had come out of it the poorer. Judged her. Lost her. 'How did you get over it?'

Mitchell breathed out and shook his head. 'You can't hate everyone forever. People make mistakes, that's human nature. But you have to let go and try make a good life for yourself or you'll die lost and lonely. It's taken way too long already. Now it's time we tried to build on the good things.' Those cool Maitland eyes zeroed in. 'Are you in?'

'Yes. Absolutely.' Max bumped shoulders with

his brother and chinked his glass with Mitch's. 'To the Maitlands. A force to be reckoned with.'

'Hell, yeah. To us.'

Jodi looked across at them and winked. 'Whoa! Brotherly love overkill.'

Knowing that there was a future for them all sent a hot buzz through him. There was still a long way to go and a lot to work through. But he had a family. Okay. Wow. Who would have known how good that would actually feel?

Gabby would be proud.

Gabby wouldn't be proud of this, though. Much, much later, Max sat on his deck in the cool night air, his head in his hands, and stared at the decimated garden. So his attention had been temporarily distracted. He hadn't watered or fed the plants for a while—he'd been busy. And, yeah, okay, he'd kept the curtains closed so he wouldn't have to see them and the bright colour that reminded him of what he'd walked away from.

But did they all have to die?

Of course they did. Just his luck. He tipped his head back and let the emotion spring free from his lungs in a long, cold laugh. Typical that not all the happy cards could be stacked in his favour. He had a family, sure, but no one to share that amazing feeling with.

No *Gabby* to share it with.

Slowly he picked off brown leaves and let them drop to the deck. Maybe it was a sign. He should throw them all in the bin and retreat to the barren landscape of his pre-Gabby life. It was colourless but ordered. Dull but predictable. Most of all it was pain-free.

He looked across the tops of the city buildings to the Sky Tower. Remembered the bravery she'd found to jump off. The risks she'd started to take for both of them. The pain she'd endured for almost half of her life. The loss. But she'd still taken her courage in both hands and followed her heart.

Maybe the dead plants weren't a sign at all. Maybe they had absolutely nothing to do with his failed relationships and everything to do with the fact that he buried himself in his job to avoid taking real risks. With his heart, and his life.

His twin was right—people made the best decisions they could at the time, and lived with the consequences.

Gabby had at least found the courage to tell him, and to make such an admission would have cost her. And yet he'd failed to even try to understand. Instead, he'd taken the route he'd always taken, judged and blamed. Refused to think things through beyond his own experience. He'd seen everything through the jaundiced eyes of his past.

Mitchell's words came back to him. Maybe he needed to stop blaming everyone else and take a chance on what he wanted. On what could actually, finally, make him happy.

He was, after all, the doctor of second chances. But was it too late even for him?

He shifted his gaze over the Auckland landscape towards the sun rising over Rangitoto. A glow of muted oranges and yellows infused the air, casting pale light over the lush green of the island. Above, the dark shroud of night gave way to a dazzling blue sky. There it was, just out of reach, waiting for him to grab it.

Damn it, it was definitely time to add more colour to his life.

What the hell? Persistent thumping on the French windows jolted Gabby from her sleep. Mad axeman? Police?

As she dragged open the curtain her anxiety hit a record high. A mad axeman might have been preferable. At least she'd have known how to react.

Her silly shaking hands refused to work and her pulse jigged along at such an erratic rate she couldn't think straight. 'Max? What the heck…?'

'Good morning, Charge Nurse Radley. I need to talk to you.' He stood in the doorway wearing a crumpled tuxedo with his black tie hanging loosely around his neck. Crisp white dress-shirt tails poked out from under his jacket. Creased, slim-fitting trousers emphasised his divine body. He looked like he hadn't slept for days. He looked ruffled and edgy. He looked…simply stunning.

Or perhaps that was just the stars in her peripheral vision. But good looks were no excuse for barging into her space.

Hell, she'd come to terms with him leaving her, and what he thought of her. She didn't like it but it had happened. And, as always, she was dealing with the fallout. Work helped. Mojitos helped more. But she was still raw. He hadn't given them time to talk things through more. He hadn't even given her the time of day.

It was bad enough that she bumped into him at work, but having him in her room again? Cruel. 'It's six-thirty in the morning on my day off. So this had better be important.'

'It is. It's a matter of life and death.' He bent

down and produced a cardboard box containing the most pathetic collection of droopy geraniums she'd ever seen. 'We need help.'

'You can say that again. It's about time you realised.' Examining the state of the plants, she moved sideways and let him in, taking care not to inhale too closely. Lord only knew what would happen if she breathed in that smell of his too. It was intoxicating. Lethal.

But he'd come here at the crack of dawn because of plants? He'd clearly joined her in the crazy stakes.

She carried the geraniums through to the kitchen and placed them in the sink. Then turned on the cold tap in an attempt at resuscitation. 'You need intensive care. Or at least they do. I don't know what I was thinking, giving you sole care of these.'

'I neglected them.' He studied her and gave her a nervous smile. 'Look, Gabby, I neglected a lot of things.'

'Oh?' Now this was getting interesting. Her heart restarted its weird axe-murderer lumpy rhythm. 'Like what?'

'Like telling you how very sorry I am that we lost our baby.' *And that you can't have any more.*

He didn't have to say it, but it was there in the

silence and in those startling Maitland eyes. She pressed her lips together to hold the hurt inside. They'd never had a chance to grieve together and come to terms with the pregnancy and the loss. Everything had happened so quickly. Including falling in love with him. 'Me too.'

He took a deep breath. 'And I neglected to tell you I understand about Joe.'

'Oh.' Her hand instinctively went to her necklace. 'Max, I don't need—'

He gently placed his finger on her lips. 'I said I understand. I really do. I've thought about the hell you must have gone through so young. I couldn't see that. I just judged you because of what happened to me. The words "adoption" and "fostering" left me cold, and I couldn't see past that. I'm so sorry. I was a jerk.'

She shrugged, trying to find words, but nothing seemed adequate. So she smiled instead. 'Yes, you were. A capital jerk.'

He smiled too. 'Gee, thanks.'

'I was only agreeing with you.'

His smile grew serious. 'I do know how much you're hurting. Losing someone is tragic. I know.' His fingers went to the diamond. 'This is something to do with Joe, isn't it?'

'Yes, it's his birthstone. I never take it off.'

'I noticed.' His eyebrows rose and she saw his eyes were warm, sparking with a gentleness that melted that hardened corner of her heart. 'That first night in the bar?'

'Was his birthday.' The day she celebrated and regretted in equal measure every year. Now the hurt meshed with the love she felt for her child and for Max. She didn't know if she was strong enough to take any more.

Then his palm caressed the necklace, stroked her throat. Heat zipped between them. 'It's beautiful. Like you.'

Her need for him was shooting off the scale. Being so close to him was torment. She stepped away. 'Max, please, don't do this. I can't take these games.'

'Will you ever stop interrupting?' He laughed and filled the space she'd left. Kissing distance. That's all. 'Hear me out, Gabby. I neglected to tell you that I'm crazy mixed-up and only just beginning to get sorted out. I'm trying, I honestly am. I wasn't looking to fall in love with you, but it just happened, and I didn't know how to deal with it. And then the ectopic pregnancy clouded everything and I was scared for you… Eugh— What the hell?'

He tapped his foot and made a splashing sound.

Together they looked down at the lake of water lapping towards their feet.

'Shoot! The tap!' Gabby jumped to the sink, where the plants bobbed forlornly. 'Great. That's all I need. You causing chaos. A plant graveyard. And now a flood. It's Armageddon. Save me from the plague of…' She paused. 'Oh, yes. Of course, I know…' Arms dripping with water, she shook her fist skywards, tipped her head back and giggled. 'Nonna! That's enough now. Stop it. Leave me alone.'

'You don't believe all that, do you? She's not really got it in for you.'

Gabby smiled. For some reason, even though he was causing chaos in her home and her heart, she felt freer than she'd ever been in her life. So phooey to Nonna. 'No. But it's always good to have someone else to blame, right?' Shoving a towel at him, she said, 'Now, give me a hand clearing up.'

Starting at the edge of the room she knelt and pressed a towel into the water, then squeezed it out into the kitchen bowl. Max knelt next to her and together they worked through to the middle of the room. Every time he dragged the towel back towards him his arm brushed against hers. Every time their skin touched she felt the same jolt of electricity she'd had the first day they'd met. Seemed nothing had changed, certainly hadn't dimmed. If anything, her feelings for him had deepened.

When he caught her eye she captured his gaze. *I love you.*

The words were there, threatening to trip off her tongue, but then his little speech before the flood began to sink in. She knelt up and pulled him round to face her, the tight knot in her throat threatening to choke her. 'Hold on. Hey, Maitland One. You love me?'

'Finally. Yes, Gabby. I love you.'

'Well, wow. That's a surprise.' She balled the towel into her fist and screwed it tighter, not knowing how to deal with the sudden lightness in her chest. And trying at the same time to be strong when tears were springing in her eyes.

'Yeah, well, it was news to me too.' He took the towel from her hands and dropped it to the floor. Then took her hands in his and held them against his chest. Water seeped up through her pyjamas.

But she didn't care. All she wanted to do was look into those eyes and listen to his voice. Soft and gentle, yet solid and strong.

'But it's the best kind of news. I'm not good at this, Gabby. You make me happy. That's all. From the minute I saw you in the pub I've been lost. In you. You've shaken me up, changed my life and I didn't want you to do that at first. I fought against it, I didn't want to love you. I lost my parents and Mitchell and I've been too afraid I'd lose you too. But now I have the love thing cooking well. And I'm working on the trust.'

Was this what she thought it was? Was this what she even wanted? This could be a chance for them both, a second chance at grasping the life they both wanted. 'What are you saying? The commitment-phobe wants to commit now? Somehow?'

He grinned. 'Yes. Yes, I do, Gabby. I know I have a long way to go, but I reckon that together we can put the hard times behind us.'

She'd never believed it could be possible. But seeing the devotion on Max's face challenged her beliefs. She could be loved. She was lovable. She could love. She just needed to let it in, and allow herself to give love too. To Max.

Just one thing stood in the way. 'But what about

babies? You know I can't have any now, and I don't want you to hold that against me sometime in the future. You have to be honest with me. And I understand if you want to walk away.' She held her breath, her pulse racing as he looked deep into her eyes.

'I know, Gabby, and I'm so very sorry. You'd make a wonderful mum. Maybe we can get help, and we can certainly look at options. Whatever you want. And if it doesn't happen for us then we'll be stronger for it.' Cupping her chin, he tilted her face to his. 'Trust me, there are enough Maitlands in the world.'

How could there ever be? She laughed. 'But I want you to have everything you deserve, and that includes a family.'

'I have one right here. That's enough for me.' At her frown he pressed a kiss on her forehead. 'Honestly.'

'Are you sure? Because I don't want you to regret—'

His mouth pressed against hers and stopped her words. Stopped any kind of rational thought. All she knew was that he was there, with her, and that was all that mattered. Anything else could be talked about and worked on. Now that they both knew how.

His kiss intensified as he meshed his fingers in her hair, crushed his body against hers. And she crushed him right back, clinging to him because this time she would never let him go. His arms held her so tightly she knew he felt the same.

He tasted sweet and dark, promising a day of sinful pleasure. And another, and another. A lifetime.

After yet another mind-numbing kiss he drew back a little and traced his thumb along her bottom lip. She caught it between her teeth, mesmerised by the heat and the love blazing in his gaze. His words came out in a whisper. 'So how about we work on it together? Slowly.'

'How slowly?' She wriggled her hips against him and nodded towards the bedroom. 'Not too slowly, I hope?'

His hands ran down her back and cupped her bottom as a dangerous glint infiltrated those Maitland eyes. 'Well, we could start with the physical…see how we go. Give me a score and we'll work on improving it. Every day. I can work very hard and I'm a fast learner.'

As he picked her up and walked through to the

bedroom she leaned her head against his chest, felt the regular solid thud of his heart. And hers jumped in sync. Whatever the future held for them now, they'd face it together. 'Sounds like a plan, Maitland One, a very good plan.'

Just like always.

A perfect ten.

Two years later...

'So Mister Five, happy birthday. How was your first day of school?' Gabby stepped into Mitch and Jodi's lounge, handed over the birthday present to her eager nephew, and couldn't hold back a smile. It was so great to see him tearing around without a care in the world.

He ripped off the wrapping paper and dithered, one eye on the playroom, clearly uninterested in the adult small talk when there was fun to be had with a new fire engine and lots of friends. 'Cool, Auntie Gabby. We had story time and a birthday cake for me.'

'Cool indeed. Now, go play with your party guests.' Gabby ruffled Jamie's hair until he dodged out of her grip. Then she went to help Jodi in the kitchen, preparing sandwiches for the hyped-up five-year-olds.

Two years had seen her and Jodi becoming fast friends, and the chances to meet up and grow into each other's life had become more and more frequent. 'He's growing up fast.'

'Way too fast. But healthy, thank goodness. There were times I didn't dare imagine he could even make five. But he's like a whirlwind. I wish I had half his energy.' Jodi stopped cutting and looked up, tired shadows lining her eyes. But they were happy shadows and for good reason. Gabby's heart did a little dance as she watched the soon-to-be mum press her hand to her bulging tummy. 'And how I'm going to manage with a baby and a five-year-old demon, I don't know.'

'Just so long as you take care and get lots of rest. And we'll be there to help.'

As Gabby spoke she heard the door latch drop, felt the familiar flicker of heat and her body's immediate response. Max was here. She wandered through to the front room, trying to keep her excitement in check. 'Hey, husband.'

'Hi, Charge Nurse Maitland. Sorry I'm late. You know what it's like. Things don't always go as planned.'

'You're here now and that's all that matters.' She curled into his waiting arms, pressed a kiss on his cheek. Then, leaning her head against his chest, she took a breath. 'I have news.'

'We got the house?' He drew back a little. 'I thought we were exchanging contracts tomorrow.'

'Yes. Tomorrow, and as far as I know that's all going well.' She bit her bottom lip, weighing up the words. For over ten years she'd shunned this—then struggled to believe it could be possible. 'Phillipe rang.'

'And?' Max's face clouded. Their journey had not been easy. Two rounds of assisted fertility had been testing on both of them, but they'd stuck through it, holding each other up when it had seemed impossible. He'd been there for her throughout, solid and determined and reliable. And had infused it all with his sense of fun and his love. Anything seemed possible with him around.

Her heart almost beat out of her chest. 'And it worked. I'm pregnant.'

'Okay. Sit down.' He steered her to a chair as if she would break at the tiniest touch. His mouth twitched into a slow smile that spread and lit up his face. 'How many eggs took?'

They both knew they had a long way to go. But she knew—felt deep in her soul—that this time it was going to be all right. This time it would work. She played with the necklace at her throat, knowing that no child could ever take the place of her firstborn, but would equally fill her heart. 'Just the one.'

'One. A baby. Our baby.' His hand tenderly touched her stomach and he gazed at her with such love she wondered how it was possible she could be so lucky. 'So definitely no multiples in there?'

'Two? Are you completely mad?' She smiled over at Jodi who nodded in agreement. 'One set of Maitland twins is enough for anyone to handle.'

* * * * *